A More Complicated Fairytale

Emily Witt

ACKNOWLEDGMENTS

The plot of *A More Complicated Fairytale* came to me in a dream, and the whole process of writing it has been similarly dreamlike. I am grateful to a great many people for helping make the dream a reality. Thanks firstly to my friend Rachel, who at this point probably doesn't even remember reading the first draft way back in early 2013 and pointed out I resolved my conflict far too quickly. Thanks also to the WIPpeteers and those who beta read for their invaluable feedback. And especially to Edy, for somehow never getting sick of all my nagging (or at least pretending not to).

The amazing cover for this book was designed by K. L Schwengel. Visit her at
http://klschwengel.com

CHAPTER ONE

"Felipe, come with me. I have bad news."

Prince Felipe, the younger prince of Nardowyn, followed his father's order. He wondered what the news could possibly be, since the King had come personally to get him. As they made their way towards the Queen's suite, Prince Felipe tried not to let his imagination run away with him, but there were few things the news could be if his father felt they ought to hear it together.

When they reached her suite, Queen Juliette was waiting. "It's Sebastian, isn't it?" she asked as they entered, referring to her eldest son and Felipe's brother. It did not bode well that the King did not respond, instead choosing to quietly usher Felipe inside and sit down.

Like every other twenty-one year old in the kingdom, Prince Sebastian was serving eighteen months of National Service, patrolling the border between Nardowyn and Gallit. While he should not have been in any immediate danger, there were still tensions between the two nations left over from a war decades prior. There was always going to be an added risk sending the Crown Prince so close.

"What's happened?" Felipe asked. "Has Sebastian been injured?"

King Gilles cleared his throat. "I'm afraid it is worse than that," he said. He took a deep breath. "The Gallits, they… Sebastian is dead."

Queen Juliette let out a strangled sob. Prince Felipe looked over at her, but he was yet to register exactly what his father had said. For a brief moment he wondered why his mother was crying, though as the news sank in, it became more apparent. A lump formed in his throat. He swallowed, feeling his cheeks heating up.

"There must be some mistake."

"Felipe…"

"No! Sebastian wouldn't… he couldn't…"

Queen Juliette stood from her seat and made her way over to him, kneeling down in front of him. She took his hands in hers and pleaded, "Felipe, you need to be brave. If your brother is gone, that makes you –"

"Oh, for goodness' sake, mother!" The prince threw her hands away and stood up angrily, nearly knocking the Queen over in the process. "Do not speak to me like I am a child!"

The Queen did her best not to react to her son's outburst, and quietly picked herself up, sitting in the chair Felipe had just left. She knew how close the two boys had always been. There had only been eighteen months between them and she had watched their mischief with quiet amusement. As time wore on, Sebastian, as the eldest, had had to put a lot into preparing to one day be King, but Felipe had always taken his brother's absences with good grace. He had no desire to be King and was happy enough for his brother to take on that responsibility, even if he did give Sebastian a good ribbing about it now and then.

Not knowing what else to do, he quickly paced out of his mother's suite. The sun streaming in through the tall windows made the room far too cheerful for the news he had just had delivered to him. He retreated back to his own room and thumped himself down on his bed.

"You idiot," he cursed the ceiling as though it were his brother. "You bloody idiot. Why would you go and do something so completely stupid?"

His cheeks became hot again and this time he also felt his eyes welling up. He didn't want to cry. Crying seemed like some kind of acknowledgement that Sebastian was gone. The longer he could deny it, the better.

Cait heard the rapid knocking on the front door and looked up, surprised. As far as she knew, no one in her family was expecting company that afternoon. A minute later, her family's maid, Sophie, appeared in the doorway of the sitting room.

"Miss Caitlin, your friend Ava is here to see you," she announced, and then ducked away into the hall.

Cait stood up to greet her friend. "Ava, how are you?"

Ava didn't answer. "Cait, have you seen the newspaper today?" she asked instead.

Cait shook her head. The paper in question was lying on the coffee table; Cait had been sorting through the day's mail, but usually left the newspaper for her father.

Ava grabbed Cait by the arm and pulled her back toward the sofa. Once they were both seated, she unfolded the paper and handed it to Cait.

"Look!" she exclaimed, her voice high pitched with worry. "The King blames Gallit for Prince Sebastian's assassination and he's declared war. Guy's going to have to go and fight."

Guy was Ava's older brother, and at twenty-one, was also performing his eighteen months' National Service. He still had twelve months to go. Cait learnt as she skimmed the headlining story that the National Service laws were going to be changed; simple border control would give way to all out conflict.

She only read the first half of the article before she looked up and asked, "Will he be home before any of this?"

Ava nodded and motioned back to the newspaper. "The King has given the Gallit Prime Minister a month to prove Gallit wasn't responsible. If he can't, then... we're at war. So I hope he'll have time to come home for a little while." She paused for a moment and slid a glance at Cait. "I'm sure he'll want to see you as well."

Cait felt her cheeks heat up. "I'm sure he'd much rather spend that time with his family," she said, avoiding Ava's gaze.

"You're not fooling anyone, Cait. I know you've fancied Guy since... oh, I don't even remember when. And he likes you, too. One of you ought to hurry up and say something!"

By the time Ava finished speaking, Cait's cheeks were a dark red. She kept her gaze firmly on her hands and only looked up again when Ava softly patted her arm.

"I'll let you know when he's home, anyway. I'd best be going now; I was already on my way home but I thought I'd drop in."

Cait walked Ava to the door and then returned to the sitting room. She tried reading the rest of the newspaper article, but she was too distracted by a fluttering in her stomach. Whether it was concern for Guy as a friend, or a giddy delight that her feelings were mutual, Cait wasn't sure.

A few days later, Cait went to collect her younger sister Ginny, and Ava's sister Bridget, from school. Speculation around the school was rife. Unexpectedly, the speculation was not about the war. The younger girls were much more interested in Prince Felipe, the death of his brother, and the situation that put him in. As far as anyone could tell, the King had no intention of protecting Prince Felipe from fulfilling his National Service duties, but he was now the only heir to the throne. He'd need to produce his own heir before he left to fight in Gallit. He'd be in more danger than his older brother, surely.

Cait smiled. The girls' concern for the welfare of a prince they'd never personally laid eyes on was endearing. Prince Sebastian had been the better-bred of the two. He had spent his entire life preparing to be King one day; the public had spent his entire life watching him being groomed for that role. Prince Felipe, on the other hand, was known for charming every woman he met, and leaving a trail of broken hearts in his wake. However, his propensity for this behaviour didn't stop many young girls in the kingdom from swooning over every picture of him that appeared in a newspaper.

"I bet King Gilles will have Prince Felipe off visiting all the princesses and noblewomen they know of to find one he likes," Bridget surmised.

"Perhaps he'll visit us," Ginny said, with a glance at Cait.

Cait raised her eyebrows and couldn't help a small laugh. "Ginny, darling, I am definitely not a noblewoman. And I'm sure that if I ever met the prince, I would probably end up insulting him and ruining any chance you may have had of being his sister-in-law."

Ginny turned away, pouting, and put on a burst of speed so that she was walking ahead of Cait. Bridget kept pace with her, and Cait simply allowed herself a small smile at the back of their heads.

Within the next week-and-a-half, several things occurred. Firstly, Prince Sebastian's body was returned to the palace and given a state funeral, attended by nearly everyone in the city. He was not buried in his family's own burial grove, but in one set aside for those who fell as a result of war. It had been Prince Sebastian's own wish that if he died as a result of his military service, he would be buried with his comrades.

A few days later, Cait received a note from Ava to say that Guy had returned home. He had six weeks before he had to return to the army. His superior officers were already preparing for potential war, but he was not required for a while yet. So far, the Gallit Government had only denied responsibility for Prince Sebastian's assassination, so King Gilles still planned on sending the Nardowyn army to war against their neighbours.

Soon afterwards (some remarked that not enough time had passed since Prince Sebastian's funeral), King Gilles announced a three-day festival would be held in a month's time. Royals and nobles from far and wide would be invited. They may have been at war with Gallit, but Nardowyn was still surrounded by three other countries. There would be balls, feasts and live performances from travelling acts. There would also be a lottery for those residents of Nardowyn who would not automatically receive an invitation, to give them a chance at an opportunity to partake in the festivities.

Two nights after the lottery had been established, with court officials beginning to draw names out, Cait and her family were invited to dinner with at Ava's house. Cait spent much longer than usual trying to decide what to wear. Meanwhile, Ginny stood in Cait's bedroom doorway and teased her. "I don't know if Guy would like that one. Maybe the blue dress instead?"

Despite her best efforts, Cait took her sister's comments to heart. She put down the mauve blouse-and-skirt set she had been considering and picked up the blue dress lying on her bed. Behind her, Ginny giggled.

In the end, Cait chose the mauve anyway. She looked in the mirror and once again pinched her cheeks to add some colour before she headed down the stairs to meet the rest of her family.

The journey only took about fifteen minutes and soon they were being greeted at the door by Bridget, who all but bowled them over with excitement.

"Look!" she exclaimed, waving a piece of paper in front of Ginny's face. "We're going to the Festival!"

"What?" Ginny exclaimed. "You've already got an

invitation?" She snatched the paper from Bridget's hand.

"Bridget, at least let them inside, will you?" called a male voice from further down the hall.

Cait thought she had managed to calm herself down on the coach ride over. However, all her nerves reappeared when Guy came towards the door and took his youngest sister by the shoulders, steering her away from the entrance so their guests could enter. Bridget and Ginny disappeared into the sitting room, still jabbering about the invitation to the Festival. Cait's parents also moved past her and down to where Ava was waiting to lead them to the dining room, leaving Guy and Cait alone.

"It's good to see you again, Cait," he said.

"You, too. I wish you were home for good, though."

"Well, the King *will* make decisions affecting the whole country while he's angry."

"But surely he can see that sending countless more young men to their deaths isn't going to bring his son back! Why doesn't he stop and consider other options first?"

Guy smiled. "Perhaps you should march on up to him and tell him."

"I'm sorry," Cait replied, feeling her initial blast of fury abate. "I'm just worried about you."

Guy smiled at her a moment longer and then to change the subject, held out his arm to Cait. "Would you care to accompany me to dinner, m'lady?"

"I'd be delighted, sir," Cait replied with a giggle, and took his arm. She would have been able to find her way around the house blindfolded, but that wasn't going to stop her from letting Guy play the part of gallant gentleman.

During dinner, Ginny and Bridget plotted how they might sneak Ginny into the Festival on Bridget's family's invitation. The adults also discussed the Festival, though they were more concerned with whether the city could cope with the inevitable crowds, and what attractions would likely be present.

When it came time to leave, Cait hung back in the hall after everyone else had left in order to say goodbye to Guy properly.

"I hope I'll see you again before I leave, Cait," he said.

"I'll make sure of it," she replied. She wondered if she ought to take Ava's advice and tell Guy about her feelings for him, but before she could fully convince herself, she heard her father calling to her from the carriage. "I need to go. Goodbye, Guy."

After that night, Ginny took to waiting patiently on the front steps after school each afternoon in the hopes that it would be the one when the postman delivered her own family's invitation to the Festival. This would mean she would no longer have to conspire to sneak in with Bridget. However, as the fortnight of the lottery continued, no invitation for their family was forthcoming.

It was on the last day of names being drawn when Cait heard the front door slam and Ginny's prolonged squeal become louder as the younger girl ran through the house.

Cait was the first person she came across and Ginny waved an envelope, complete with the Royal Seal, in front of her sister's face. "We're going, Cait!" she exclaimed. "We've been invited to the festival! We might even meet Prince Felipe!"

Cait took the invitation from Ginny's hands to have a look at it herself, at the same time attempting to bring her sister back down to earth. "Ginny, princesses from three different kingdoms are going to be there, as well as every noblewoman in Nardowyn. Prince Felipe is going to be quite occupied meeting all of them; he won't have any time for us.

"You never know," Ginny replied and Cait just smiled, deciding not to argue.

By the time the invitation arrived in Cait's household, the Kingdom was becoming very busy as travellers from far and wide arrived in the city to prepare for the festival. While some came in caravans, many required rooms at the local inns and soon there was barely a vacancy to be found. The site of the festival was the palace grounds and the grounds of the two neighbouring estates. When Cait walked Ginny home from school each afternoon, they could see stalls, tents and stages being erected on nearly every available patch of ground.

Finally the opening day of the festival arrived. Cait had to admit that Ginny's excitement was infectious, and even she was looking forward to trying new foods and seeing the shows. Cait's family met with Guy and Ava's and they walked the rest of the way to the Palace together. In their excitement, Ginny and Bridget kept getting too far ahead and having to wait for everyone else to catch up.

They arrived at the palace at around ten o'clock on the festival morning and discovered a queue from the gates that was leading halfway down the road. Riflemen in dress uniform stood on either side of the gate to repel uninvited guests. Cait and her family waited nearly an hour before they reached the top of the line; Ginny was practically bursting with anticipation by the time their invitation was stamped and they were each given a token to carry with them throughout the day, designating that they were allowed to be on the grounds.

Guy took Bridget and Ginny's hands and bent down slightly so that he was at their eye-level. "All right, where shall we go first?" he asked.

Ginny and Bridget both looked around wildly. "I don't know!" Ginny finally exclaimed, and tugged on Guy's hand. "Let's just go this way and see what we find!"

CHAPTER TWO

"Your Highness, are you ready? You're going to be late!"

In his bedroom, Prince Felipe rolled his eyes. "Just another minute!" he called back to the guard on the other side of the door, and bent down to reach under his bed. He pulled out a brown cloak that was hidden there and stood again, fastening it around his neck. When it was secure, he crossed the room to his window and opened it.

"All right, I'm ready now!" he called out. The guard pushed open the door just in time to see the Prince's head disappear as he climbed down the trellis outside.

"Your Highness!" the guard exclaimed, running to the window and leaning over the windowsill. Prince Felipe looked up at him from halfway down and grinned.

"If the public gets to enjoy all the fun at a festival being held in my honour, why should I miss out?" he shouted up to the guard. "Tell Her Highness I apologise for my absence at lunch!"

As he continued to descend, he heard a clamour as the first guard was joined by a couple of others who blamed him for the prince's escape. He then heard the argument as they decided how best to deal with the situation. Prince Felipe knew from experience he had about seven minutes before the guards would get downstairs, find their colleagues and commence a proper search. By then, he could well and truly have blended into the crowds that were flooding onto the grounds for the festival.

Sometimes he wondered why the trellis outside his window was never removed; he never made any effort to hide the fact that he was using it. Perhaps his parents didn't mind because it gave the men in their employ something to do other than just take shifts protecting the palace grounds. Either way, Prince Felipe certainly enjoyed the chase and wasn't going to complain as long as he was able to keep getting away with doing it.

He jumped the last couple of feet to the ground and raised the hood of his cloak over his head. As he began walking away, he recognised the blonde maid who was working in the garden. He often chatted to her when he was out like this. He gave her a friendly bat on the arm as he passed. She started but then grinned as she turned and saw who it was.

The prince turned so that he was walking backwards, and grinned back at her. "Send them in the wrong direction for me, won't you?"

"As always," she replied.

"That's my girl!" Prince Felipe waved and then turned around and broke into a jog towards the rows of tents and pavilions ahead of him. He slipped between two of them and wove himself in amongst the anonymous strangers on the other side, simply becoming part of the crowd.

From the moment they had set foot inside the palace grounds, Ginny and Bridget had dragged their older siblings around various displays, stalls and performances. One of the vendors offered the opportunity to dress up in

Aufaron traditional costume: brightly coloured, full-length dresses with puffy sleeves and symbolic embroidery for the women and girls, and vests with similar embroidery for the men and boys. Ginny watched the flashbulbs going off and wanted to have a go herself. Upon looking at the price, Cait realised it would be one of the more expensive attractions they were going to encounter, and suggested they see how much spending money they had left at the end of the festival. Begrudgingly, Ginny agreed.

It was when they were considering what to purchase for lunch that Ava and Cait ended up separated from Guy and their sisters. Ava and Cait were inspecting the options from a man selling noodle dishes, but when they turned around, Guy, Bridget and Ginny seemed to have been completely swallowed up by the crowd.

"They were just over there!" exclaimed Ava, pointing to the stall where the other three had been looking at food. "Where could they possibly have gone?"

"It's all right," said Cait, briefly trying to figure out a way to balance her plate of food in one hand so she could put the other on Ava's shoulder. She gave up on that idea and instead simply said, "I'm sure they'll be fine. Maybe they couldn't see us through the crowd and thought *we'd* wandered off. Guy will look after them. And they know where to meet us at the end of the night, so they'll find us there if not before. Come on, let's go and find somewhere to sit and eat."

There was an area with tables set aside nearby. As it was the middle of the day, it was crowded, but Ava and Cait timed their arrival to snap up a table just as a husband and wife vacated it. Cait wanted to savour her meal - the noodles and vegetables had been cooked in a spicy sauce she'd never tasted before and she wanted to make it last - but she and Ava agreed they should eat as quickly as possible to free up the table again. After Cait assured Ava a second time that Ginny and Bridget would be fine, they decided to go and wander some more of the attractions.

Truth be told, Cait was actually worried about Ginny, and hoped she was still with Guy. There was little chance of them running into the others in these crowds, though, so she was hoping for the best. Before they had parted ways with their parents, they had arranged a meeting spot for the end of the day's festivities so they were certain of all making it home together. Cait simply crossed her fingers in hope that everyone would be reunited when the time came and there would be nothing to worry about.

Towards the middle of the afternoon, they came across a wooden stage with a banner across the top bearing the words 'Alfonso the Magnificent, Grand Illusionist'. On the stage, a man was describing the great feats of illusion that the crowds would witness when the show started in ten minutes. Neither Cait nor Ava had ever seen a magic show before, so they bought tickets and found themselves good seats.

For the next three-quarters of an hour, they witnessed mind-reading, card tricks and even a woman being sawn in half! Even Cait had been on the edge of her seat for that finale.

When Alfonso the Magnificent had taken his final bows and disappeared from the stage, Cait turned to Ava. "What did you think?" she asked.

"That was spectacular!" Ava replied. "How do you think he did that last one?"

"There were two women in the box," said a hooded man who had been sitting on Cait's other side. "That's the only way it could be done."

"Do you think so?" Ava leaned across Cait a little to speak to the man and in doing so, recognised the face under the hood. She sat back again, quickly. "Cait, it's -"

The cloaked man held up a finger to quickly quiet her. "Please don't give me away. I'm trying to avoid my guards at the moment."

He lowered his hood and Cait realised why Ava had been so surprised. She looked at Ava. "Well, won't Ginny and Bridget be jealous?" She looked back to Prince Felipe with a wry smile. "Our younger sisters are big fans of yours, your Highness. We tried telling them it was unlikely any of us would see you here, but they kept their hopes up. I'm sure they're going to be frightfully upset about this."

"Well, I suppose you were right to discourage them. I'm not supposed to be spending my time at magic shows designed to entertain the masses. In fact, I believe I should be dining with the Princess Royal of Brellalan at this very moment."

"Then why aren't you?"

Cait didn't mean to ask such a direct - and perhaps slightly accusatory - question, not to the prince, but it was out of her mouth before she could remind herself who she was talking to.

The prince did not seem too perturbed, though. "Have you ever had to spend time with women who have been raised only to aspire to one day marry a prince?"

"I can't say that I have, Your Highness."

"Then count yourself lucky. I would much rather spend my time at magic shows in the company of such charming ladies as you and your friend, than dining with any of them."

As he spoke the words, a yell was heard behind them, and the prince looked up with a start. Someone shouted "There!" and a group of red-uniformed men of the palace guard pointed towards Cait, Ava and Prince Felipe.

Glancing back at Cait and Ava, the prince quickly stood and replaced his hood over his head. "It's been lovely," he said with a nod, and then leapt across three benches and off in the opposite direction to the guards. They shouted again and ran after him, but Cait saw him quickly blend in with the crowds and silently wished the guards luck. They were probably going to need it.

Cait and Ava turned and looked each other, both processing the conversation that had just taken place. Ava raised her eyebrows. "Well, Prince Felipe thinks we're charming," she said.

"Yes," Cait replied. "But did you hear the way he talked about those poor princesses as though they were dirt under his feet? Poor girls. One of them will probably have to end up married to him."

That afternoon, Cait and Ava saw a dance show from the Kingdom of Iberrang and found another food vendor selling hot food, some of which they purchased for an early dinner. At half past seven all the guests were ushered to the parade ground in front of the palace, which had been kept clear of tents or stages. After a display from a group of riflemen in dress uniform, the crowd was treated to ten minutes of fireworks.

Once those were over, Cait and Ava made their way to the agreed meeting point, and both of them breathed a sigh of relief when they saw Guy and the two younger girls already waiting.

"Where did you two get to?" Guy asked when they got closer.

"We could ask the same of you," Ava replied, giving him a friendly shove.

"We turned around and the three of you were gone," Cait added. "We've been worried all afternoon."

"Well, we've survived," Guy assured them.

"What exciting things did the three of you find after we left?" Ava asked, eyeing the carry bags that both Bridget and Ginny were carrying.

Ginny thrust one hand into her bag and pulled out a small wooden doll. She held it up by a string coming from its head. "Look!" she said, and pulled a string hanging between its legs. The legs and arms flipped upwards, making the doll look like it was performing a jumping jack.

"Did you do anything fun?" Ginny asked.

Ava slid a glance at Cait, who smiled slightly and shrugged. "Well, we saw a magic show and met Prince Felipe," Ava declared as casually as she could.

Both Bridget and Ginny's eyes widened for a moment

before narrowing in scepticism. "I don't believe you," Ginny said emphatically.

"It's true," Cait added, wearing a playful grin. "But it's all right, girls, he was horrible, you wouldn't like him."

"Well, I certainly don't believe *that!*" Bridget exclaimed, crossing her arms and pouting.

Ava laughed. "It's all right, Bridget. I don't think he was as bad as Cait says."

"Did you really meet him?" Bridget asked.

"We did," Ava said. "It seemed he was running away from meeting princesses."

"And what did he think of you two?" Guy asked.

"Apparently, we're charming," Cait replied with a quirked eyebrow.

"He didn't even seem to mind when Cait started scolding him," Ava added.

"*Cait!*" Ginny moaned. She looked mortified, as though Cait insulting the prince might have blackened her own name in some way.

"Well, that certainly sounds like Cait," Guy replied. "No man is safe."

A few minutes later, their parents finally met them and they began their walk home. Ginny and Bridget showed off their purchases, and then excitedly told their respective parents about their older sisters' run-in with the prince. Once Ginny had mentioned all the details she was already aware of, she turned around to Cait to ask more questions. By the time they were halfway home, there was little else Cait could tell her, but that didn't stop Ginny. Cait was relieved when she could close her bedroom door behind her and put an end to the interrogation.

Prince Felipe's guards had finally caught up with him later in the afternoon, and he was duly marched back into the palace. He waited patiently while his father ranted at him for skipping the lunch with the princess of Brellalen and then returned to his room to begin preparing for dinner.

A knock came at his door just as his attendant was adjusting the lapels on his dinner jacket. It was Carmen, the woman who had been nurse to both the princes when they were younger. Even when they had outgrown her services, she was considered enough of a family friend that she had been given her own apartment in the palace. She and Prince Felipe had always been particularly close; he had always found her much easier to talk to than any members of his family, with the exception of his brother.

"I hear you've been getting into trouble again," she remarked, settling herself into an armchair on one side of the room.

Prince Felipe sent his attendant away and sat down on the edge of his bed to put on his boots. "Why should everyone else get to have fun while I have to sit through stuffy lunches?" he asked, pouting slightly for effect.

Carmen smiled slightly. She was used to this sort of ranting from him. "Well, what did you get up to out there? I want to hear all the details."

The prince sat up, one boot still waiting to be put on, and looked Carmen right in the eye. "I met a girl down there," he said, and the older woman raised an eyebrow at him. "Well, two, but one in particular. All I know is that her name is Cait. Even after she realised who I was, she just kept on talking to me the way she had been. I think she even got angry at me at one stage. Mother Above, do you know how *refreshing* that was, Carmen? I could talk to her the same way I talk to you."

Carmen's expression was hard to read. The prince thought it lay somewhere between amusement and concern at his enthusiasm about a commoner he had only met briefly during one of his running away episodes. He wondered if he ought to assure her that the encounter meant nothing in the grand scheme of things, but the thought of saying that aloud depressed him. Instead, he concentrated on putting on his remaining boot.

"So, are you likely to see this girl again, between the young ladies you're *supposed* to be meeting?" The prince frowned and she added, "I really don't think you ought to upset your father anymore. It's already caused him a lot of stress after having to deal with the King and Queen of Brellalen this afternoon."

"I don't suppose so," Prince Felipe said. "It was just a chance meeting after all. I doubt I'll see her again."

He had finished with his boots, and he stood up, making sure a broad smile covered his face. "Would you accompany me to dinner, Carmen?"

She smiled back, well aware that he was putting on a show. "I would be honoured."

.

CHAPTER THREE

On the following two mornings, Cait and Ava's families used alternate entrances to the festival grounds so they could ensure they saw all the attractions they missed on the first day. They ate more food than they thought they could fit in their stomachs (taking advantage of copious free samples), saw more dancing and even a performance by a contortionist. They purchased souvenirs like hand-dyed silken scarves and small toys and ornaments. Since she still had spending money remaining, Ginny decided to go back to the Aufaron pavilion where the children had been dressing up in the national costume. She posed for the camera and then, while she was changing back into her own clothes, Cait gave the gentleman manning the stall their address so that he would be able to send the photograph once it was developed.

On the final day, everything finished earlier than it had the previous two nights. There was to be a ball for the visiting royalty and the nobles of Nardowyn, so it was a case of all hands on deck inside the palace and no one would be available to supervise outside. It also meant visitors could begin packing up in the daylight and make an early start for home the following morning.

There were no fireworks this time, as they would have lost their effect in the daylight, but King Gilles and Queen Juliette, along with Prince Felipe, stood on the palace steps as the crowd gathered to hear what the King would say to conclude the festival. The other royal parties were sitting on benches that had been placed along the top steps, in front of the grand ornate doors.

Knowing that this would be the last chance they would have to get anywhere near as close to Prince Felipe as Cait and Ava had, Ginny and Bridget ensured that they got a spot close the front. Even Cait had to admit that Prince Felipe did look handsome in black tie and tails. She watched as he leaned over to a nearby guard and pointed to a spot in the crowd quite close to where she and Ginny were standing. The guard nodded and made his way down the steps and into the crowd. Cait lost sight of him then, until he reappeared at her shoulder, causing her to jump with surprise.

"The prince requests your presence at this evening's ball," he informed her. He spoke stiffly, as though he personally disapproved of the message he was delivering, but knew he had no choice but to deliver it.

Cait blinked. "What? But…"

"His Royal Highness insists."

"I…" Cait was at a loss. If the prince was requesting her presence at the ball, she couldn't very well refuse, and yet she had no idea what he would want with her. They had only spoken briefly after the magic show two days before; surely she hadn't made that much of an impression! She looked back at the guard, unable to come up with any other excuse to say no. "Tell his Highness I would be honoured."

The guard nodded, and made his way back up to the prince. They spoke briefly, and then Prince Felipe looked directly at Cait, a large smile on his face. Cait couldn't bring herself to return it.

Ginny and Bridget turned to her with wide eyes.

"Prince Felipe wants to see you again!" Ginny exclaimed.

Cait was far too busy processing the conversation she had just had to point out to Ginny that she was stating the obvious.

"Seems you made an impression on him," Guy remarked. Cait couldn't quite read his expression, but that didn't stop her turning red and averting her eyes from him.

A few minutes later, two pages sounded a fanfare on trumpets and the crowd steadily quieted. King Gilles held up his hands to silence the last lingering murmurs and then he began to speak.

"Ladies and gentlemen," he announced, "I'm afraid it is time to end our festivities." There were a few comical moans from some of the men in the crowd, and the rest of the guests chuckled.

The King continued, "My son has met many of the young women in attendance tonight and has gotten to know some of you..." Here the King nodded to the princesses behind him, but then also cast a glance at some of the young women at the front of the crowd. "I hope he behaved himself, ladies." The girls giggled, and many of the other guests laughed again.

Prince Felipe took the jab with good spirits and moved to his father's side, placing a hand on King Gilles' shoulder. "Father, I promise I have been on my absolute best behaviour," he declared, but followed the comment with a wink at the same group of girls as though sharing some intimate secret with them. The girls giggled again.

Cait rolled her eyes.

The King continued his speech. "Felipe will meet with our visitors once more at this evening's ball and then he will consider the decision before him, choosing one lucky lady to be his bride. There will, of course, be an official announcement as soon as he makes this choice. Until then, I thank you all for coming, and bid you all a very fond goodnight."

Cait had hoped she might be able to slip away

unnoticed rather than being forced to be present at the ball, but it was not to be. The same guard as before appeared at her side again, and after Ava and Guy promised they would see Ginny safely back to her parents, Cait saw no option but to follow him. From the main entrance hall of the palace, they took a side door and Cait was left in a small antechamber. She looked around awkwardly for a few minutes, wondering what she was supposed to do now, until a middle-aged woman in a long red dress burst into the room.

"Oh, my dear, I'm so sorry," were her first words to Cait. "I thought I had raised him better than this."

"Pardon?"

"You'll have to forgive Felipe, he acts on his whims without any regard for how that might affect anyone else. My name is Carmen, dear. Yours?"

"Caitlin."

"Lovely to meet you, Caitlin. Now, if Felipe is insisting you attend this ball, you'll need something to wear. Come with me."

Cait had no idea where she was being led, though soon the ornate ceilings and artworks lining the walls disappeared, and they were in a much simpler part of the palace. There were no portraits of past royals staring down at Cait, and the walls were just stone. Finally, Carmen stopped and opened the door on an enormous wardrobe. On one side hung several suits and sets of men's evening clothes. On the other, a supply of dresses and ball gowns. Cait couldn't think of a feasible reason why the Royal family would require such a stock, but she didn't question it. She was just relieved she wasn't going to look as out of place as she felt.

Carmen selected a few gowns she thought might fit Cait and between the two of them, they carried the garments into an adjoining room.. There was a full-length mirror in one corner, as well as a screen to change behind, and a couple of chairs as well. Beside the mirror was a small dressing table. Lying on it were both dress pins and hair pins, along with a few assorted hair pieces.

The first dress Cait tried on was a shade of blue that she adored immediately, but unfortunately, it was too tight around the waist. She had a similar issue with a red and black one, but finally, there was a deep plum-coloured one that fit almost perfectly. The sleeves were a bit loose and fell off her shoulders, but Carmen managed to fix this with a couple of well-placed pins.

Once she was dressed, Carmen looked Cait up and down and then eyed her hair dubiously. "I'm afraid I'm not much good with curls," she said. "I've never had any need."

"Would it do as it is?" Cait asked nervously. She had simply fastened it in a ribbon that morning to keep it off her face. Even like that, it still extended a fair way down her back.

"I think it could," Carmen said. "We should probably get you in there. Felipe will be expecting you. Come, I'll show you the way."

Carmen led Cait back through the maze of corridors and then to the entrance of the ballroom. "I'll have to leave you here," she said apologetically. "I hope you can at least enjoy yourself a little."

"Thank you for your help," Cait said. As she watched Carmen disappear back the way she had come, she wished she could run away as well. However, the guards on either side of the door were already looking at her expectantly, so she edged her way into the ballroom. A few people looked her way, but when they didn't recognise her, they simply looked away again. Cait wasn't surprised. Many members of the Nardowyn nobility were there, but Cait's family, as respectable as it was, did not move in those circles.

By the time Cait arrived, the ball was already well underway. There were several couples dancing, accompanied by a string orchestra in one corner. A long table covered in food stretched along one side of the ballroom, and many guests were standing near it, small plates in their hands. The King and Queen were not dancing, but watched the proceedings from two thrones set on a platform at one end of the room.

Cait stood by herself in one corner, wondering where Prince Felipe was. If he wanted to talk to her again, she hoped he would do it soon so she could escape the awkwardness of her current situation. As the current dance ended, she finally caught sight of Prince Felipe as he bounded up the stairs to speak briefly to his mother. When he turned around to face the crowds again, his eyes scanned the guests present until finally they alighted on Cait.

As the orchestra prepared for the next piece, he made his way towards her, brushing aside other prospective dance partners and, Cait surmised, probably offending three different nations in the process.

"Cait, isn't it?" he said when he reached her.

"Yes, Your Highness. Short for Caitlin."

"May I have this dance, Cait?"

"Your Highness, I'm not really one for dancing, I really think..."

"Nonsense, I insist." He held out his arm and Cait was left with no choice but to take it. He led her right to the centre of the ballroom and then other couples filled in the space around them. The musicians began playing a waltz, and Cait tensed as Prince Felipe put one arm on her waist. It had been a long time since she had really danced at all, and when she had, it had been with Guy. This was not how she had imagined returning to such an activity.

"Are you nervous?" the Prince asked, a glint in his eye as though the notion pleased him.

Cait hesitated before answering, "A little, your Highness. I wasn't exactly expecting to be here and I don't know *anyone*."

"You know me."

"I hardly think that's the case."

As they danced, murmurs from the other guests followed them around the dance floor. Cait could only wonder what they were saying. The Prince noticed also and grinned at her.

"We seem to be causing quite the stir," he remarked.

"Indeed," Cait agreed. "Surely Your Highness shouldn't be wasting his time dancing with me when there are so many more fitting ladies in attendance."

"Perhaps I'll choose you to be my wife and horrify everyone."

Cait understood the spirit in which the comment was meant, but it didn't stop her from bristling at the implication that marrying her would be "horrifying".

"You know, though," Prince Felipe continued, "I somehow get the feeling that you would say no. There's nothing stopping you, of course, it's just that, well, few women would object."

"Your modesty astounds me, your Highness."

"I'm not being conceited," the prince argued, "but marrying a prince, particularly one who is, as of a couple of months ago, heir to the throne, is about as high as you can go."

"And I suppose that's all a girl would ever think of? Status? Wealth?"

A slow grin spread over the prince's face. "Oh, I see what it is," he said. "You've already got someone, haven't you? A stable boy or a woodcutter's son or some such? Your family disapproves but you know that it's true love and you're just waiting for the right moment to run away together."

Cait shook her head, almost laughing at the ridiculousness of the prince's scenario. "You are far from the truth, your Highness," she said. "But yes, there is a man…" She trailed off, not really wanting to share everything about herself and Guy with a stranger.

The prince slid a glance down to Cait's left hand, which was sitting on his forearm as they danced. "But there's nothing official?"

Cait averted her eyes. "No... he's in the middle of his National Service so he'll be going to war soon... but when he comes back, perhaps..."

Trailing off, Cait looked back up at the prince again and was surprised to see that his expression was not condescending as she had expected but understanding and sympathetic.

He was still looking at her like that a few moments later, even when the music ended and he had released her from his hold. Those who had been dancing applauded their musicians and then began to seek out new partners, or moved to the side if they did not want to participate in the next piece.

"It was a pleasure," Prince Felipe said, inclining his head towards Cait. "I'm afraid you are correct, I do have certain obligations and I can't really spend more time with you, but thank you for agreeing to come tonight. I had hoped I might see you again, and when I saw you this afternoon..."

"The pleasure is mine, Your Highness," Cait replied, giving a smile she hoped was convincing.

"You'll have to excuse me now, though. There are a few ladies here I am expected to dance with." With that, he left Cait standing in the middle of the dance floor and approached one of the ladies Cait assumed to be a foreign princess (and a potential wife for Prince Felipe).

The ball continued, and Cait found herself unable to avoid dancing with some of the other gentlemen present; the prince had managed to draw their attention to her. They insisted on asking her about her family and where she was from; she answered the same few questions several times throughout the night, and got the same responses when they realised she wasn't as important as they had assumed. It was frustrating, but she put up with it out of politeness.

Finally, several hours later, the ball came to an end. Cait was unsure what she was supposed to do until one of the royal guards approached her. He led her back the way Carmen had taken her earlier, and soon they found Carmen waiting with Cait's dress outside the room she had used to change. The guard waited outside while she changed back, Carmen assisting in removing the pins and doing up the buttons on Cait's own dress.

Once she was ready, the guard led her back to the front of the palace, where a coach had apparently been ordered especially to take her home. They waited a few minutes before it arrived, and Cait gave the driver her address before the guard helped her into the carriage. He gave her a small bow and closed the door.

On the trip back to her house, Cait reviewed the evening's events. Prince Felipe had said he wanted to see her again though she couldn't think why. She must have made a bigger impression on their first meeting than she thought. But then he spent their entire conversation interrogating her, making her feel like she was on a witness stand rather than at a ball. Nothing seemed to make sense.

Though it was late, Ginny had been allowed to wait up for Cait, and she practically pounced on her older sister the second she walked in the door of their home. Ginny wanted to know all the details about the ball: did Cait dance with Prince Felipe? Who else was there? What was it like inside the palace? Cait described it to the best of her ability and wished she could share Ginny's excitement. She had already been tired from spending the last few days on her feet, but the added confusion of Prince Felipe's attention compounded all of this, and she realised how much she wanted to just fall into bed. Eventually, Ginny's questions died down, and upon the reminder that she actually had to get up for school the next morning, she made her own way to bed, allowing Cait to do the same.

CHAPTER FOUR

It was nearly a week later when the word started spreading through the city: Prince Felipe had chosen a bride. Her name was Maria, and she was the eldest daughter of the King of Aufaron. It was a perfectly suitable choice and no one could be happier.

Apparently the Prince had been every bit his charming self when proposing; he had asked the princess to accompany him on a walk through the palace gardens and then while she had been taking a rest on one of the many secluded benches scattered throughout the grounds, he had gone down on one knee and presented her with what had been his grandmother's engagement ring.

"Well, I'm happy for them," Cait declared one afternoon a few days after the announcement; she and Ginny were in the sitting room, and she was brushing Ginny's hair. "Now it's only a month and all the fuss will be over."

"Cait, was Prince Felipe really as bad as you make out? Most girls would be so excited to have that chance. Why not you?"

Cait shrugged. "I suppose I just didn't find him as charming as all the other girls seem to. Everyone seems to think I should have considered it a huge privilege that he asked me to the ball."

"Well... he is the prince."

"Oh, not you as well, Ginny."

They were interrupted at that moment by a knock on the front door. It was a postman, with a letter from Guy and Ava's parents. They were inviting Cait's family to dinner with them and some other friends to farewell Guy before he returned to the army. Upon reading it, Cait felt a sinking feeling in her stomach. She had known his leave would eventually come to an end; she just wished it hadn't come so soon..

They arrived at Guy's parents' house that Friday evening and were greeted by Ava, who ushered them inside. There were a few other families already there, some of whom Cait recognised. Guy was speaking to a group of men, some his own age and some closer to that of his father, so Cait spent the time until dinner talking with Ava and some of the other women.

Cait hopes she would be able to see Guy alone but wasn't sure if she would have the opportunity with all the other people there. However, Guy saved her the trouble of having to engineer some time alone with him by inviting her out into the small courtyard at one side of their house after dinner. Cait sat down on the small bench there, and watched, concerned, as Guy paced impatiently in front of her for a minute. He then finally settled down beside her.

"Guy, what's the matter?"

"You mean apart from the fact that come Monday I will be on my way to a fully-fledged war, rather than just having to patrol the borders and making sure no one untoward gets past?"

"Well, apart from that." Cait gave him a small smile that she hoped was comforting. She wanted to keep the mood light.

Guy turned slightly to properly face Cait. "Will you

miss me, Cait?"

"Of course I will! What sort of question is that?" She leaned sideways towards him and nudged his shoulder with her own. It was something he would often do to her in a gesture of friendship.

"I'm glad to hear that. Will you write to me then?"

"Of course. Every day, if you want."

"It will be a welcome relief to hear from you."

"You have to promise you'll write back to me, then. So I know you're still all right."

Guy nodded. "That sounds like a fair deal."

They fell into silence after that, until Guy suggested they head back inside before they were missed. For the rest of the evening, Guy was occupied with talking to the other guests, and Cait didn't get another chance to talk to him until her family was leaving. Her father and mother both shook Guy's hand and his father's, and then they ushered Ginny quickly outside. At the same time, Ava and her father seemed to find something that urgently required their attention in another room, and suddenly Guy and Cait were on their own.

Guy looked in the direction his sister and father had just disappeared. "Well, that was subtle," he remarked, a small smile on his face.

Cait chuckled softly and then took a deep breath. "This is it, then," she said. "On Monday, you're going to war."

Guy nodded sombrely. "Cait, if I come back, will -"

"*When* you come back," Cait cut him off firmly.

"All right, *when* I come back, would you consider… I don't know, going to a dance with me or letting me take you to dinner?"

Cait's shoulders had tensed as Guy began the question, but relief swept over her as she finished it. She laughed, a wide smile crossing her face. "I would love to. I thought we were going to reach a point where I would have to ask you."

Guy's relief was also obvious, and he laughed, too.

"Well, why didn't you? It would have made it so much easier for me."

Cait absently reached up to straighten his collar. "Well, you did fine in the end. I must go, my parents will be waiting. Promise me you'll stay safe."

"I will."

"No unnecessary rushing into battle."

"I'll do my best."

"Good." Cait bit her lip. "Well, goodnight."

"Goodnight, Cait."

The next month passed in an ordinary enough fashion, though the city was once again becoming crowded and hectic the closer Prince Felipe's wedding became. Finally the day arrived and Cait found herself being dragged out of their house by Ginny at what Cait considered to be far too early an hour for a Sunday morning.

"We have to get a good seat!" Ginny exclaimed, not sounding even slightly apologetic.

Early as it was, large crowds were already lining the streets that led from the palace to the town hall. Cait and Ginny found a spot on a corner; Ginny was able to squeeze to the front, but Cait hung back; as long as Ginny was within her sight, she wasn't worried about how well she could see the wedding party herself.

A few hours went by before anything happened. Cait had struck up a conversation with a family she was standing next to when she heard Ginny and some of the other younger spectators begin exclaiming that the prince's carriage was on its way. An ever-nearer roar of cheering from the crowd further up the street confirmed their claims.

As the carriage drew level with her, even Cait had to admit that Prince Felipe looked dashing in his wedding regalia. He wore a long coat in a deep shade of purple and underneath was a beautifully tailored waistcoat in a lighter shade. A silver-topped cane lay across his lap, and on his head sat a small gold crown that was traditionally worn by the heir to the throne on such occasions.

All around Cait, people were waving flags and cheering and Cait found herself joining in; the atmosphere was infectious. Prince Felipe waved to the crowds on both sides of the street, even blowing kisses to a few of the girls. Cait stopped cheering when she saw that and shook her head; one would hardly have thought the man was going to his wedding.

That carriage soon disappeared around the corner further up the street and it was another hour or more before any more excitement occurred. Finally the bride's carriage appeared, causing even more excitement than the prince's. Everyone was straining to catch a glimpse of the princess as she passed; those who couldn't see were asking what her dress looked like and how she was wearing her hair. Cait saw just enough to see that Princess Maria looked very beautiful and graceful, every inch a future queen.

When Princess Maria had also disappeared around the corner, Ginny wriggled her way back to Cait. "I suppose you want to wait out here until the wedding is over and you can see them returning to the palace together?" Cait asked her.

Ginny looked sheepish. "I would like to," she admitted, d "but you look tired."

"You got me out of bed too early and I've been squashed amongst strangers ever since," Cait complained then added, "No offence," to the family she had been speaking to earlier. The father of the family smiled and shook his head, indicating none had been taken. His daughter had been at the front with Ginny and was now telling him excitedly about what she had seen from the edge of the street.

"Maybe if we went home quickly, mother could come back with me in time to see them return to the palace," Ginny suggested.

Cait laughed softly. "Mother is quite happy to wait for the photographs in tomorrow's newspaper, remember? She's not up to being on her feet for hours just to catch a fleeting glimpse of the prince as he passes."

Ginny looked torn, and Cait felt guilty for trying to convince the younger girl that it was time to go home, especially when so many of the other spectators were clearly staying until after the wedding ceremony.

"All right," she said, rolling her eyes. "Hopefully the wedding won't take long. Go back to your spot; we'll wait."

Ginny's eyes lit up and she immediately started wriggling her way back through to her spot on the street's edge. Cait smiled. She could manage with an extra hour or two on her feet if it meant her sister would be happy.

The wedding service itself must have only been short because it was only a little over an hour before the cheering began again, this time coming from the opposite direction. Princess Maria had joined her new husband in his carriage. Prince Felipe had one arm around her, and they both wore large smiles as they waved. Cait found herself smiling and waving back. Even if she didn't swoon over the prince the way so many other girls did, there was no denying he looked very happy now. There was no point in being cynical about that.

The following day, the newspapers all ran photographs of the prince and princess sharing a kiss on one of the palace balconies. Ginny laid claim to her family's copy soon after it had been delivered, sighing about how romantic it was and bemoaning the fact that they had not been near enough to witness that particular moment. Cait pointed out they probably would have had to camp out in the cold to get a decent spot that close to the palace and that seemed to at least make Ginny thankful for small mercies.

Now the prince and princess were off on their honeymoon, though the destination had been kept a secret. Speculation was rife; had they gone to Aufaron to visit Princess Maria's family as man and wife, or would they have ventured north to the beaches of Brelallan? Perhaps it would be west to the rainforest and bungalows of Koamwen? Though the newspapers continued to debate the issue for at least a week, the truth was no one actually knew. The newlyweds had left the palace under cover of darkness, and even though many papers claimed to have had someone keeping look-out, every one of these scouts seemed to have seen something different.

The honeymoon lasted for three weeks, and the couple arrived home amidst much fanfare. Their skin was several shades darker than it had been when they left, finally answering the question of their destination. Clearly a great deal of time had been spent at the beach in Brelallan.

Now that they were home, they were expected to return almost immediately to their royal duties. Princess Maria would be expected to mainly concern herself with charity work and patronage, while Prince Felipe was to begin concentrating on training for the war in Gallit; it was only six months until he would embark on his own eighteen months of National Service and it was assumed that he would hold a rank of some authority. As such, he was expected to know what he was doing. Prince Sebastian had been training to go into the army from a young age, and had thus been more than prepared when he turned twenty-one. Everyone knew, however, that Prince Felipe lacked the direction for his future that Prince Sebastian had had, but now the King was determined to ensure his son was prepared for what lay ahead.

CHAPTER FIVE

Cait had not assumed - and indeed, had not even slightly suspected - that she would have remained in the prince's mind almost two months after they had danced at the ball. It came as a great surprise to her, then, when a royal carriage pulled up outside her house and the coachman informed her that the prince wished to have an audience with her at the palace.

Cait and her mother had stared at each other for a moment, before Ellen started ushering her back inside to get her suitably dressed. The clothes she had been wearing would have been presentable if they had had company at the house, but she needed something better to visit her country's heir to the throne. Once she had changed her clothes, Ellen sat her down at her vanity. Despite the usual tendency of Cait's hair to misbehave, her mother managed to secure a section across the top with an ornate comb of her own, which at least gave it some semblance of having been worked on.

"Off you go." Ellen ushered her out the bedroom door and before she knew it, Cait was rushing back down the stairs. It took about twenty minutes to reach the palace, at which point the coachman helped her out of the coach, led her up the main stairs and through the doors. She was told to wait where she was, then the coachman disappeared back out the main door. Cait took a deep breath and looked around. On the night of the ball, she hadn't had an opportunity to get a closer look at the ornate ceiling and the murals that covered three of the four walls. She was still looking at them when a door at the other end of the room opened and Prince Felipe himself appeared. A smile broke out over his face when he saw Cait waiting there.

"Caitlin! I'm so pleased to see you! Please follow me." He held the door open for her and motioned for her to pass through to the corridor beyond. This she did, and then waited for him to join her on the other side and close the door behind him.

They began walking in silence, until Cait could bear the suspense no longer. "Your Highness, how did you find me?"

"I sent the same coachman to find you who took you home from the ball. He's known for his memory."

"Were you planning this even then?"

"Perhaps." He was smiling slightly, but Cait didn't take any comfort from this.

The prince seemed to realise this, because he added, "If it makes you feel any better, no, I wasn't planning anything at all. It was a happy coincidence. I suppose you didn't think I'd remember you?" Cait shook her head and he continued, "It's not often someone in my position meets someone like you who is unafraid to speak her mind as you did when we met. I hoped you might come here often and talk with me. I need something to keep my brain from rotting away entirely."

"Talk with you? About what?"

Prince Felipe shrugged. "Your family. My family. Politics. What books you've read, where you've been recently... Whatever you like. Anything you say will be in the strictest confidence, I assure you."

"Why can't you talk to your wife about such things?"

Prince Felipe stifled a laugh. "My wife was raised to be the perfect wife for a prince. In that, she succeeds very well, I'm sure, but I saw very early on she is unwilling to think a thought or have an opinion that wasn't mine first. I'm sure some would say that is as it should be, but I need someone to stimulate my mind."

Cait was not entirely sure how she should feel about being the one who would provide this stimulation that the prince apparently required. She decided it would be best not to say anything in response.

At this point, they reached a large wooden door that the prince pushed open. Beyond was an area set out with lush armchairs and velvet carpets, and further inside were floor-to-ceiling shelves stacked with thousands of books. Cait couldn't help it; her eyes widened at the sight. One wall of the room was lined with large windows letting the sunlight stream inside, and the whole room smelled of older paper and leather binding. Cait had visited the library at the university where her father worked, but even it didn't compare to this.

The prince noticed her looking around, and grinned. "Welcome to our library. Come in and sit down." He held out a hand to indicate that Cait should make her way inside and then followed, closing the door and settling himself in one of the armchairs. Cait allowed herself another look around inside, before following his invitation and sitting down in another chair across from him. Between them was a coffee table with several expensive-looking books strewn across it. Cait only recognised one or two of the titles, and wondered whether any of the others might be worth looking up.

"What did you want to talk about today, Your Highness?" she asked after a few moments of silence. The small quirk at the corner of the prince's mouth indicated he had recognised the sarcasm in her question, but she was learning that she could get away with a lot without bothering him too much. Her spiteful side was willing to push the limits.

"Tell me about your family. Your father teaches at the university, does he not?"

Cait nodded. "He is the Dean of Students. He began as a professor there, yes; he taught history. But he has been there a long time now."

"And do you have siblings?"

"I have a sister, Ginny. She turns eleven in a month."

"But no brothers?"

"No, it's just the two of us."

"Are you provided for should your father die?"

Cait wondered why the prince would ask this, and was sorely tempted to tell him it was none of his business. Instead she said, "Perhaps if the kings who ran our country were to change the laws so that my mother, or Ginny and I could inherit our father's property, it would not be a cause for my family and me to worry."

To her surprise, the prince let out a snort of laughter. Indignation rising inside her, she asked, "Did I say something funny, Your Highness?"

"Surely, Cait -"

"Caitlin."

The prince cocked his head to one side. "Very well, Caitlin. But surely you don't think your own upbringing, or that of most other women in the kingdom, would prepare you to manage property the way your father does?"

"My father studied history, your Highness, not economics or property law. Does that help him any more than the music or the languages I've studied?"

"But your father has the *mind* for it, that's what I mean."

"And who is to say I don't?" Cait responded hotly. "Or any of my friends? Are men really born with innate skills that women lack, or are we all just brought up to think this and not to question it?" Cait realised that she had raised her voice, and took a breath to regain her composure. "Has it never struck you as strange, Your Highness, how even the Goddess we worship is reduced to being a benevolent mother who guides us to the afterlife and takes care of us there? How good of her to fulfil the same womanly duties every woman down here is expected to. Surely she's capable of more than that?"

"What an interesting interpretation. What do you think our Mother Above should be doing then?" The prince's tone made it obvious he was toying with Cait.

"Did you really invite me here because you wanted to talk with me?" she asked. "Or because you find it amusing to bait me into argument?"

Prince Felipe regarded her silently for a moment before replying, "I will not deny that I do find some of what you say entertaining, but I hope you will not take this as an insult. I really do enjoy your company. As I have said before, it is refreshing." Cait wasn't how to respond to that and so remained quiet. Prince Felipe stood up. "Perhaps you have had enough for today, however. Shall I show you out?"

He offered his arm to Cait and she stood and took it, though she did so stiffly. As they left the library, the prince called for a servant to send word that a carriage should be sent to the main door to meet them. He led Cait back through the corridors they had walked earlier and to the front steps. A few minutes later, the carriage met them and Prince Felipe assisted Cait to step inside.

"I hope you will not object to returning here again?" he asked, continuing to hold her hand lightly so that she could not quite get away from him completely.

"Of course not, Your Highness," Cait replied, knowing there was no other response she could give. She tried to accompany her answer with a polite smile, but wasn't confident that she was successful in that endeavour.

He nodded. "Until next time, then," he said, and stepped back so the footman could close the carriage door behind Cait.

She had been at the palace for less time than it took to

travel there, and yet it had been enough for her. The memory of the prince laughing at a belief she held dear still stung, and the idea of having to return to the palace for similar "conversations" in the future did not improve her mood. She wished she had told him she didn't wish to come back. After all, she'd been rude to him earlier; what difference would one more outburst have made?.

Having been given no indication otherwise, Cait assumed that the carriage would arrive at much the same time the following week, and was prepared to the point of only needing to lace up her dress before she was ready to leave. This time she managed not to lose her temper with him with the prince. He told her some stories about his brother, Prince Sebastian, and their childhood, and Cait found herself sharing similar ones about herself and Ginny.

Cait realised quickly, though, that the prince was clearly unaware of the privilege he had been raised in and she found herself feeling inadequate in comparison. Prince Felipe didn't seem to notice her discomfort, however, and went on talking about family holidays and the school teachers his father had hired from various far-flung places in the same way. Eventually, Cait was sure he was deliberately doing it to annoy her.

While their conversation lasted longer this time, she still left the Palace feeling frustrated and wondering how she could possibly get out of what was clearly going to become a weekly engagement. She moaned to her mother and Ginny when she arrived home that evening; Ginny gave her very little sympathy, which Cait rather expected, and offered to go in her place the following week if it was such a problem. Her mother at least seemed to understand why she was upset. Neither of them, however, could think of anything that could be done.

As time went on, however, another reason to dread these visits to the Prince began to surface, one that even Ginny would have had trouble refuting had Cait explained it to her. It had been four months since Prince Felipe had married Princess Maria, and there was yet to be any news that they were expecting a child. Rumours began circulating that perhaps the princess was unable to conceive. Added to that, Palace staff unable to hold their tongues had let it be known all over town that the prince was inviting a young woman to visit once a week. It didn't take much longer for the townspeople to begin assuming that they knew exactly what was going on, on those Tuesday afternoons that Cait visited the Palace.

Soon after that, they had figured out that it was Cait specifically that the Prince was seeing. Once that was the case, Cait could feel people staring at her every time she left the house. One day she had been planning on going out with Ginny, only to discover a reporter who had been waiting on the steps, poised with a notebook and pencil, ready to bombard her with questions. Her mother, thankfully, put paid to that plan by slamming the door in his face and sending Cait back into the house. It was only when she was sure Cait was out of sight that she opened the door again and, after some heated words (which Cait listened to from the top of the stairs), Cait didn't think they'd be seeing that particular writer again.

The next time she visited the Palace, she tried explaining to Prince Felipe why her visits were becoming so difficult a task for her, but apart from facetiously offering to send one of the Palace guards around to watch her house and to follow her around whenever she went out, he showed little concern, and quickly changed the subject.

"What did you mean last week when you said you thought women should inherit the crown? Surely you didn't mean that?"

"Why wouldn't I have, your Highness? So much of the actual governing of the kingdom is left to the King's advisers, is it not? In Gallit, they allow female representatives in their Parliament. Would a woman's rule really go all that astray every now and then?"

The Prince's face clouded on hearing Cait speak of Gallit admiringly, but he did not answer immediately. Over the past few months, they had engaged in several arguments of this nature, and the prince was slowly beginning to see Cait's point of view on the subject of her gender. She knew there were certain things he would never agree with her on, and the possibility of women succeeding the throne was probably one of them, but the fact that he was at least thinking about it made her feel she had made some progress.

At the beginning of the following week, there was a letter from Guy awaiting her. The further she read, the darker her cheeks became until she wanted to crawl under the nearest table and die a swift death.

Dear Cait,

We've been hearing rumours around the camp for a while that Prince Felipe has been wooing a woman other than his wife. I asked Ava about this last week and she tells me there's no wooing involved, but the woman who has caught his attention is you. I know you can look after yourself, Cait, and that you would never let him attempt anything untoward, but I have to ask, what exactly is it he wants with you?

Yours in morbid curiosity,

Guy.

Ginny ducked her head into the sitting room and, seeing that Cait was reading the letter, joined her on the sofa. "What does Guy say today?" she asked.

"Oh, nothing," Cait replied, folding up the letter quickly before Ginny could see any of the writing. "The same things he usually writes about."

Ginny looked at Cait with concern. "What did he say, Cait?"

"He…" Cait bit her lip, wondering whether or not to share the contents of the letter with Ginny. "Oh, Mother Above, Ginny. I hadn't told him about how Prince Felipe insists I see him every week; I didn't know what he'd think. But there were rumours in the camp and he asked Ava about it... so now he knows. He must think I'm some kind of harlot. What do I say to him?"

Ginny looked at Cait sideways. "Well, just tell him the truth. Don't you think he'll believe you?"

"But..."

Ginny snatched the letter out of Cait's hand and read it quickly. "It doesn't seem like Ava said anything horrible about you," she decided. "He probably wants to hear it from you as well, just to be sure." Ginny stood up and took Cait by the arm, dragging her up from the sofa as well. "Come on, go and find paper and a pen and write back to him."

Cait couldn't help a small laugh as Ginny pushed her out of the room. She went upstairs and obtained paper and a pen as instructed and then made her way back down to the sitting room to write her reply.

Dear Guy,

I had been hoping you wouldn't find out about this. I didn't know how to tell you I had the prince insisting I come to the palace every week without it sounding suspicious, especially as I knew there would be rumours flying about. I can assure you there is nothing untoward going on; mostly we just sit in the library and talk. (You should see the Palace library!) Well, we usually end up arguing, and I have a feeling the prince delights in making me angry. Sometimes he seems all right, but so often I leave feeling exhausted and frustrated. I hope you won't think less of me for keeping this from you, and I hope that this reaches you before you become in any way convinced by the rumours you hear.

Yours always,

Cait.

She sealed the letter and addressed it, and then put it on the small table in the entrance hall to remind her to post it the following day.

CHAPTER SIX

Cait had not been at the palace long the following week when she and Prince Felipe heard Princess Maria's voice from outside in the hall. "Felipe? Where are you?"

"In here," the prince called, and the door opened. The princess looked as though she had been about to say something important, but her expression changed when she saw Cait in the room, and she held back.

"Oh," she said, "don't let me disturb you." She turned quickly and retreated from the library. For one brief moment, Cait thought that the prince was going to call his wife back, and that she would be allowed to go home early. This was not the case. Cait felt a pang of sympathy for the princess, and turned back to the prince.

"Can't you see that my presence here upsets your wife? No doubt she has heard exactly the same rumours about me that I hear myself. That can't be pleasant for her."

"She has nothing to be jealous of."

"No, but as I have tried to tell you before, she is not the only one who wonders. And you're not exactly helping matters. We're always alone in here; I doubt you've ever even considered some sort of chaperone for our chats. Word gets out quickly, Your Highness. Your staff know more about what goes on here than they may let on, and they don't hesitate to pass it on to others."

The prince's face clouded. "I know what my reputation was like before I married; I gave people every reason to talk about me then. But I resent your implication that I am not a man of honour and that I have not changed since I married."

"Your Highness, sometimes it takes more than a few months of marriage to change an entire public's perception of you. You've made it even harder by sending a royal carriage to bring a young woman well beneath your station to the palace once a week because you enjoy *talking* with her."

The prince frowned again. Though it was clear he wanted to disagree with Cait, it seemed he could find no way of doing so. Instead, he looked back at her and said curtly, "I've had enough for today. You may go."

Cait stood and curtsied as usual, then made her way out of the library. All the way back to her home, part of her felt smug for putting the prince in his place and finally getting him to understand her concerns regarding their weekly meetings. Another part of her feared the consequences she would suffer had she truly offended him. She had not taken him to task on an issue this personal before.

When she arrived home, she found her mother and Ginny sitting silently in their sitting room. Both of them avoided her gaze when she entered, even as she looked from one of them to the other for an explanation.

When none was forthcoming, she asked for one. "Mother? Ginny? What has happened? What's wrong?"

Ginny raised her eyes to meet her older sister's gaze and that seemed to be the last straw for the eleven-year-old. "Oh, Cait!" she exclaimed, springing from her chair to wrap her arms around her sister's waist. Cait returned the embrace, and deepened the questioning look at her mother over Ginny's head.

"Cait, we just heard from Guy's father..." Her mother trailed off.

A sinking feeling settled itself in Cait's stomach, but she told herself not to let her imagination run away with her. "What did you hear?"

Her mother took a deep breath. "Guy has been killed. He was shot by the enemy."

Cait felt like the world was suddenly slowing down around her. Sounds became dull or muted and she was only slightly aware of her own movements. She pulled Ginny's arms from around her waist and slowly moved across the room to sit down.

Ellen sent Ginny to find a servant to bring a pot of tea. When it arrived, Cait accepted the cup and drank from it with only a dim awareness of the taste as it went down her throat. Cait didn't have dinner with the family that night and no one objected. She took herself up to her room and curled herself up into a small ball on her bed; only then did she allow herself to cry. Her body shook as she sobbed, and it was in that state that she fell into a fitful sleep.

Cait had no interest in the details of the battle in which Guy had been killed, but she did learn from Ava that many men had died and it was deemed too far a distance to try to return them all to the city for burial. Their last rites were performed by a priest attached to the military and they were buried on an agreed site far enough away from the war zone to be left undisturbed. A memorial service was organised for the following Tuesday so that the families and friends of the fallen could have a chance to say some kind of farewell to their loved ones.

On the Tuesday morning, Cait wrote a letter of explanation for Prince Felipe and left it with one of the family's maids. Later that afternoon, she and her mother made their way to the funerary grove where Prince Sebastian and men fallen in previous wars were buried.

The area was surrounded by towering trees that had been cultivated over decades; the only gap in the trees was filled by a wrought iron gate made to look like branches curling to the sky, except for those nearest the female figure just to the right of the lock. She represented the Mother Goddess, and her creations bent towards her in admiration.

Cait caught sight of Ava, Bridget and their parents and they made their way towards each other. Ava's eyes were red and puffy. Cait held her hand throughout the service, and felt Ava's grip grow tighter as a small plaque with Guy's name on it was uncovered and his name read out.

When the service was over, Cait gave Ava and Bridget a hug each, and tried to remain composed. As much as she had admired Guy, she felt that she didn't have the same right to cry over his passing as his siblings did. She didn't take up too much of their time; there were other people in attendance who wanted to offer their own condolences.

A few days later, Cait made her way back to the funerary grove. The plaque with Guy's name on it was surrounded by flowers that had been left by the family, but Cait knelt down and laid a small bunch she had brought alongside the others. She reached out and traced the letters of his name. The stone was cold, and still damp with morning dew.

"I don't know if you ever saw my letter," she said, "but there's nothing between the prince and me. I always wanted to be with you." She paused and blinked back the tears that had welled in her eyes. "Mother Above, I wish you were still here."

Cait looked up sharply and wiped her eyes when she heard a twig break behind her. Turning around, she saw no other than Prince Felipe, the same brown cloak he had been wearing the day they met fastened around his neck.

"I thought I might find you here," he said when he saw Cait looking at him.

Cait felt a cranky knot form in her stomach. He was the

last person she wanted to see, especially here. "What are you doing here?" she asked, looking away angrily.

"I came to pay my respects," he replied.

"Oh, really?"

"Yes, actually." For the first time, he sounded as though her cynicism of him bothered him. "I know this man meant a lot to you and I know how you must be feeling."

"It seems to me you are very rarely aware of how I'm feeling, Your Highness, why would now be any different?"

Cait saw the Prince bristle and look away, and wondered if she was being a bit harsh. She wanted to be alone, though, and despite her crankiness, she was reasonably sure she made a good point.

After a few moments of silence, the Prince began speaking, though he did not look at Cait. Instead he kept his gaze fixed in front of them both. "You may remember that it was my brother's death that started this whole war in the first place." His voice was quiet and even. "I sat at his grave for days, just as you are doing now, and I would do anything to bring him back."

Cait immediately felt guilty for her earlier outburst; in the time she had known prince Felipe, she had always been so determined to feel annoyed by him that it had never occurred to her to consider how he might still be dealing with Prince Sebastian's death; that he might even still be mourning.

"I'm sorry," was all she managed in response a few moments later.

"Will you walk with me?" He offered Cait his hand and she took it, standing up. He led her towards a bench not far away, under a tree. As they walked, he continued, "I know how I come across to you, Cait. Flippant, careless, probably even a bit selfish. The thing is, when you're in my position, you receive less judgement for being a spoilt prat than for admitting that perhaps you have any kind of feelings."

"Were you close? You and your brother?"

They reached the bench and Prince Felipe motioned for Cait to sit down, and then followed suit himself. In response to her question, he nodded. "Sebastian had friends from university, but, well, I was never really the studious type. He kept an eye on me, kept me company..." He smiled sadly. "Though I suppose most would say he didn't do a very good job of keeping me out of trouble. Sebastian was always the perfect son, a good heir to the throne. I still felt like I was in his shadow so I had to find ways of getting out into the light."

"So you chose getting your name in the headlines as much as possible."

"Perhaps not the best course of action, but it worked. Even if it was for the wrong reasons, I got as much attention as he did."

"And now? The act doesn't seem to have changed much, apart from there being fewer young women involved." The prince smirked, and Cait found that she was smiling, too.

"Now?" he replied. "Now I've suddenly got a future as King thrust upon me. I can't let anyone think I might be worried about that."

"Are you worried?"

"What on earth do I know about being a King?" He sighed. "Part of me almost hopes I die on my National Service, too, and that ruling the country will be left to my child."

"You shouldn't say things like that," Cait chided him. A moment later, it registered what he had said and she asked, "Your child? Does that mean..."

He turned to look at her quickly, alarmed. "Oh. I'm not supposed to tell anyone yet. The doctors said to wait a few more weeks to be sure before making any announcements. But you can keep a secret, can't you, Cait?"

"Of course."

"Then I can confirm that my wife and I are expecting

our first child in May."

"Congratulations, Your Highness."

"Thank you." He was silent for a moment, before adding, "I'll still be away, but I suppose I can be granted leave when the happy day arrives." He sounded apprehensive more than anything else.

"Of course," Cait replied, not knowing what else to add.

The prince turned to face Cait properly. "It's good to be able to talk to you like this, Cait. Perhaps we should be more honest with each other more often."

To her surprise, Cait found herself agreeing. "If you'd always been like this, perhaps I wouldn't have dreaded coming to visit you every week."

"Do you dread it so much?"

"Well, yes, to be perfectly honest with you. And I don't think I've ever really kept it a secret. You've just never listened!"

She noted that Prince Felipe did have the decency to look apologetic. He seemed about to say something when they both heard the sound of leaves crunching to one side and looked up to see Ava coming down the path towards them. Ava stopped short when she realised who was sitting with Cait. Cait glanced between them and then beckoned Ava over, hoping Ava wasn't going to turn on her heel and disappear. Ava came closer with some trepidation.

"Your Highness, this is my friend, Ava. Guy was her brother. Ava, this is His Royal Highness, Prince Felipe."

"I'm very sorry for your loss," the prince said, holding his hand out to Ava. Ava shook it briefly, but Cait could tell she dropped it as soon as she could.

"Thank you, your Highness," she muttered, before turning to Cait. "Cait, we... we started going through Guy's things yesterday..." She paused and glanced at Prince Felipe, and Cait also wondered if he needed to be there to hear what Ava had to say. Sensing both pairs of eyes on him, the prince took the hint and stood up.

"That's my cue to leave," he said. "Cait, will I see you next week?"

To her surprise, Cait found herself nodding, rather than taking the opportunity to object. "Of course."

Prince Felipe nodded. "Farewell."

He did not walk back the way he had come, but instead made his way slowly towards the other end of the funerary grove, seemingly studying some of the other headstones along the way.

"What is he doing here?" Ava exclaimed in a loud whisper. "You didn't... you didn't *invite* him, did you?"

"Of course not!"

Ava looked around. "Does he have anyone with him? Or does he just waltz through town on his own not caring if anything happens to him?"

"He does... stupid things like that sometimes." Ava raised an eyebrow at Cait. "All right," she amended. He does it a lot."

"Not to mention stupid things like ruining my best friend's reputation."

"Yes. That, too."

Cait actually couldn't help a small smile in response to Ava's indignation on her behalf. She looked up to see where Prince Felipe was now, and saw him kneeling on one knee at the base of the proper grave sites at the other end of the grove. It took Cait a moment to realise that that it was Prince Sebastian's grave; she had forgotten the older prince had wanted to be buried with his comrades. She wondered what Prince Felipe was thinking as he knelt there.

"Cait?" Ava's voice broke through her thoughts.

"Sorry," she said. "You came to talk to me about something. What was it?"

"As I said, we started going through Guy's things. We found this." She pulled a sheet of paper out of her purse and passed it to Cait. "He never got a chance to finish it."

Cait unfolded the paper. The writing on the inside was

in Guy's hand, but the final sentence was unfinished.

Dear Cait,

You don't know me as well as I thought you did if you think I'd listen to gossip about you before I heard your own side of it. Though of course, I expect you to fill me in on all the sordid palace gossip you have accumulated by the next time I'm home.

Speaking of coming home, I should have some leave in the next few weeks. I certainly look forward to seeing your face ag…

The ink at the end was smudged, as though he had put the pen down in a hurry. When she finished reading, Cait folded the letter again and only then realised she was crying. She looked up at Ava and saw that she was very close to tears, too. The direct look from Cait seemed to be all it took to break the dam.

"Oh, Cait!" Ava exclaimed, flinging her arms around Cait; Cait returned the embrace immediately. "What are we going to do? I miss him so much!"

"I know," Cait replied. "So do I." She felt this wasn't a very useful response but under the circumstances, it was all she could come up with.

The two friends held each other for a few minutes more, before pulling away, each drying their eyes on their sleeves as they had nothing else. Ava's face was flushed red and Cait was sure she looked the same. She looked around, and realised that Prince Felipe had disappeared. Cait's first thought was that at least that meant she wouldn't be on the receiving end of any teasing about puffy, red eyes. Then she remembered their earlier conversation and decided he probably would have been good enough to not mention it.

Ava sniffed and wiped her nose again. "I should go," she said. "Mother will be expecting me home soon."

Cait stood up. "I'll come with you," she said. "I've been sitting here long enough."

She and Ava linked arms, each girl supporting the other out of the funerary grove.

CHAPTER SEVEN

As Cait waited for the prince's carriage to collect her the following Tuesday, she started feeling nervous. While their conversation in the grove certainly made her dread their meeting less, she had at least always known what to expect before. Now she wasn't so sure; it had turned out Prince Felipe could surprise her.

He met her in the entrance hall as usual. Apart from greeting each other, they walked in silence to the library. When the prince opened the door and ushered Cait through, she saw that one of the leather armchairs was already occupied. For one startling moment, Cait thought that they had interrupted the Queen, but then she realised that it was Carmen, the woman who had helped her prepare for the ball.

"Cait, this is Carmen, my former nurse," the prince introduced. "Carmen, this is Caitlin."

"Hello, Caitlin. So nice to see you again." Carmen stood and held out her hand, which Cait shook.

"Again?" Prince Felipe looked between them. "Have you met?"

"Well, someone had to look after poor Cait the first time you insisted on her catering to your whims." The prince still looked confused, so Carmen further clarified, "the ball, Felipe. Who do you think helped Cait get ready?"

"Oh, of course," Felipe replied and then looked at Cait. "I thought perhaps you were right, and someone should be here as a chaperone."

Cait resisted the urge to exclaim "Finally!" and instead gave Carmen a gracious smile. Carmen returned it and then made her way back to her chair, sitting down and picking up a book from the coffee table.

Prince Felipe motioned for Cait to sit in her usual chair and he sat across from her. Cait waited for him to start the conversation as he usually did, but this did not happen. He was sitting forward in his own chair, one hand on each knee, looking expectantly at her. She had no idea what he was waiting for her to say and the silence stretched on.

"Perhaps we were better at this when we were busy arguing with one another," she said eventually.

The prince laughed, nodding. Cait realised he had quite a nice laugh when he wasn't being scornful.

"I had been wondering," he said, "if there was anything else you wanted to see around the palace. We're always in here, but there's so much else to see. Galleries, gardens…"

"Actually, I've always wanted to have a better look in here," Cait said. "You say we're always in here but we never come much further than the door."

"Of course!" the prince exclaimed happily, though he almost immediately became unsure of himself as he looked towards the rows of bookcases behind them. "Is there anything in particular you'd like to see?"

"I'm sure you've got all sorts of hidden treasures in here that no one ever sees."

"Why don't you show Cait our copy of *The Mother's Word?*" Carmen suggested.

"Oh, yes, good idea. Follow me, Cait." They stood and the prince led Cait down one of the rows of shelves. As they walked, he explained, "I'm ashamed to admit I'm not really that familiar with most of the contents of these shelves. I read the things my tutors made me, but I don't come here of my own accord much."

"If I had a library like this," Cait replied, "I don't think I'd ever leave."

By now they had passed the taller shelves and had reached a row of smaller wooden cabinets that lined the back wall. The prince ran his hand along them, scanning the labels, until he found the one he was after. Finally, he opened a drawer and carefully pulled out a volume, placing it on the top of the cabinet. He opened the cover and then moved slightly to give Cait more room in front of it.

"Have a look through," he said. "But be careful. It's fragile."

Cait touched the inside of the cover with one hand, taking in the wonderful scent that accompanied such an old copy of their religion's sacred text. There was no title page; the words spoken by the Goddess to her priestesses in ancient times began on the first page.

"This is *handwritten*," Cait murmured in quiet awe.

Prince Felipe nodded. "It predates even our earliest printing presses."

"That makes me scared to touch it." Cait removed the hand she had had on the cover, but then plucked up the courage to carefully turn the page. On the following one was a beautiful illustration of of the Goddess creating a sprawling oak tree, her hair and her long skirt billowing behind her. The page was lined with a gold border which glinted in the light above.

Over the next few minutes, Cait carefully leafed through the rest of the book, taking in the illustrations and beautiful penmanship. When she got to the end, she looked up and saw that Prince Felipe was watching her, a small smile on his face.

"It seems I have found your weakness."

"Which is hardly fair," Cait replied. "You always seem to have some advantage over me."

The prince simply chuckled as he put the sacred book

away. Cait wanted to spend the rest of the afternoon amongst the shelves and asked if there were any more treasures she might see. Prince Felipe led her to another cabinet, where a collection of old coins, both from Nardowyn and the other kingdoms, lay on a bed of black velvet.

"This place is as much a museum as a library," Cait remarked. "It's a shame no one really gets to see it."

"We have to conserve it for future generations," the prince replied. "It's all part of our history."

"What's the point of conserving the history if no one gets to experience it?"

Prince Felipe eyed her with a small smirk for a moment before replying, "Is this to become our new topic for heated debate? At least when we're not arguing the pros and cons of women on the throne?"

"Don't worry," Cait assured him. "That will still come up."

"I've no doubt."

While Cait could have happily stayed in the library all night, all too soon it was time for her to head home. As they said farewell, Prince Felipe promised her that there would be plenty more for her to see the next week. She had a wide smile on her face as she was driven back to her house, and wished these more enjoyable visits could have begun a lot sooner.

On the following couple of visits, Prince Felipe took Cait through some of the galleries scattered throughout the palace. There were artworks of former monarchs and their wives and children, as well as depictions of famous battles and other important historical events. There were also pieces of jewellery on display, as well as various crowns worn by members of the Royal Family on special occasions. Not many commoners got to see them as closely as Cait did.

After that, Prince Felipe introduced her to the gardens, but not the ones which she had seen from the carriage window before. The gardens at the back of the palace, only ever seen by the Royal Family and their guests, were far more elaborate. The stairs led down to a lake, beyond which lay flower beds in geometric patterns surrounding an enormous, immaculate hedge maze. At the entrance, Prince Felipe challenged Cait to find her way to the centre. Thinking it couldn't be too hard, Cait accepted. She was fairly certain she got at least halfway before having to admit she was lost. She wandered a few more pathways before concluding that her best option was to sit down and wait for someone who knew the maze better than she did to come and find her.

When Prince Felipe and Carmen found her half an hour later, it seemed like the prince was trying to give her a look of pity, but he was barely able to contain a grin.

"I'm sure it would be too much to expect you to feel sorry for getting me into this mess?" Cait asked as she rose to meet them.

The Prince's eyes widened in feigned innocence. "Me?"

Cait shook her head, her lips quirking into the beginnings of a smile. She moved closer to the Prince and jabbed a finger in his chest. "Had I tried to say no to your challenge, you would have made it clear I had no choice in the matter."

Prince Felipe let himself grin then, and nodded. "Very probably." He leaned closer to Cait. "You were never going to say no, though, were you? Admit it."

Cait held his gaze for a moment, but inwardly frowned as she felt her heart speed up from his closeness. She took a step back and was able to let her smile return. "Well, I never could resist a challenge," she agreed.

"Let me show you how it's done," Prince Felipe offered, holding out his arm for Cait.

Cait could tell he had been waiting for this opportunity to show off, but it didn't bother her so much as it once might have. She took his arm and with ease, he led her to the middle of the maze. In the centre was a small garden bed full of rosebushes, though it was the wrong time of year for them to be in flower. A little while later, they headed back out of the maze and emerged on the outside in half the time it had taken Cait to get even halfway in.

"I promise you, I am never going near a maze again," Cait swore as they were saying goodbye.

"I'll convert you yet," the prince countered.

"Is that another challenge?"

"Perhaps. Are you resisting?"

Cait smiled. "I'm working on it.".

About six weeks had passed since that day in the funerary grove when Cait arrived at the palace to find the staff all in a flurry. They were rushing back and forth, putting up decorations and bringing extra supplies to the kitchen.

When the prince met Cait in the entrance hall as usual, he explained, "A combined birthday and farewell party for me. Apparently I'm getting quite the send-off."

"So soon, really?" Cait asked. That particular date had snuck up on her rather quickly.

"Twenty-one on Thursday, and then a week to prepare before I'm called up, the same as every other young man in the kingdom." He was trying to sound casual, Cait could tell, but a slight tremor in his voice exposed his apprehension. He stopped walking and turned to look at her. "I suppose next Tuesday will be the last I see of you for a while."

He changed the subject quickly after that, and it didn't come up again that afternoon, though it preyed on Cait's mind for the rest of the day. It was clear it was all Prince Felipe was really thinking about, too. Their conversations primarily consisted of small talk, and were punctuated with long periods of silence.

On her way home, the concern in the Prince's voice echoed in Cait's head and she wondered what she could possibly say or do to alleviate some of that when she saw him for the last time before he left. Her mind wandered to the horrors that probably awaited him, and she had to stop herself dwelling on all the awful scenarios her mind was only too happy to create for her. It was as she pushed away the image of Prince Felipe lying in a hospital, injured and lonely, that it occurred to her what she could do. By the time she got home, she had made her decision.

She was sitting at dinner with her family, trying to find the best time to tell them, when her father looked at her directly and said, "Cait, whatever it is that's making you fidget like that, please get it off your chest so we can all eat in peace."

Cait had not realised she was fidgeting at all, and she felt her cheeks go red under her father's gaze. Still, she maintained eye contact with him as she said, "I want to be a nurse."

Her father's eyebrows went up very quickly and Cait heard the clatter as her mother dropped her cutlery.

"And what has prompted that?" her father asked.

"I want to help," she said. "They've been desperate for nurses ever since the war began."

This was true enough. It was not compulsory for women to enlist in one of the nursing corps in the same way all the men in the kingdom were required to do their eighteen months' National Service. In the seven months since the Nardowyn army had marched on Thendem and engaged in active warfare, their casualties had increased significantly and the Nardowyn hospitals on the border barely had enough staff to deal with the influx. In spite of this, there was little that could be done to entice more women to join the ranks voluntarily.

"Cait, there are plenty of other women who can go," her mother said.

"But not enough! It was all right before, when the army was just patrolling the borders, but we've been at war more than six months now. It's far more dangerous. There are so many more risks for the men out there."

"I saw in the papers today that it's next week Prince Felipe leaves. This sudden decision doesn't have anything to do with him, does it?"

At this suggestion, Ginny let out a loud giggle, but she quietly went back to her dinner when she was glared at by both her parents and her sister.

"Of course not!" Cait exclaimed, but then under her father's scrutiny added, "Well, perhaps a little. What if I had been there when Guy had been shot? There were so many men injured that day, Guy probably just missed out on treatment that could have saved him. What if I were the difference between another man surviving or not? Wouldn't that be worthwhile?"

The entire table was silent for a while. Cait held her breath as she waited for a response. Part of her wanted to say she was going to enlist in the nursing corps regardless of what her parents said, but she knew she would never go without their approval.

"Your heart is set on this, I can tell," he father said finally. "Go into town tomorrow and sign up. But Cait... just be careful."

"It's not as though I'm going off to war. The hospitals will be far away from any actual fighting."

Her father watched her for a moment before saying quietly, "It's not the war I'm worried about."

This was when her mother spoke up. "James, you surely can't mean -"

"Ellen, we can't keep our daughters locked away forever."

"I'm not saying that! But Cait doesn't have to go off to war to avoid feeling confined."

"Please don't argue!" Cait interjected. "Mother, I'm sure I'll be perfectly safe. This is important. I want to do it."

"Your mother and I won't stop you, Cait."

Cait nodded gratefully at her father, but saw that her

mother was still looking doubtful.

The following day, she made her way into town to put her name down on the official nurse's register. There were a number of forms she had to fill out, so she was stuck in the tiny office for quite a while. The attendant, a girl about the same age as Cait, chatted happily to her as she worked her way through the papers

"They'll be glad to have you coming," she declared. "There's a large group finishing their rotation soon. Some of them are staying on longer but not all, so they're going to be desperate. You might have to learn a bit on the job, though; you won't have time to receive much training beforehand."

The thought of that made Cait's hand hesitate above the paper, but then she thought of the apprehension in Prince Felipe's voice as he spoke of going off to war and she continued writing. When she was done, she handed everything back to the girl behind the desk. She stamped a few of the papers, and then she told Cait that unless she heard otherwise, she should be back there the following week with her things, ready to leave. Cait gave her a smile and told her she would, and then she headed home to begin packing.

She knew she ought to tell the Prince of her decision when she saw him the following week, but finding a way to do so proved difficult. She knew he would try to talk her out of it, and given how far they had come over the past few weeks, she didn't really want to spend their last afternoon together arguing.

In the end, it wasn't until she was nearly back at the front door to take the carriage home that she turned to him and blurted, "I've signed up to be a nurse."

Prince Felipe blinked. "You what?"

"I enlisted. I leave on Thursday, as well."

"Cait, that's madness. Why?"

"Well, someone's got to keep an eye on you while you're away, don't they? It might as well be me."

Prince Felipe gave a small laugh, but did not look convinced. "I know you won't listen to me," he said, "but I'll say this anyway. Don't go, Cait."

"It's too late now. And besides, they need me. They've been short ever since the war began."

Realising there was no point in arguing, Prince Felipe sighed. "Just stay safe, Cait."

"You, too."

For a moment neither of them knew what to say. While it did not break the silence, Cait held out her hand to the prince, so that at least they weren't just awkwardly staring everywhere but at each other. The Prince took her hand and she expected him to simply shake it, so it surprised her slightly when he raised it to his lips and kissed it lightly. She felt herself blush and hoped the Prince didn't notice. If he did, he didn't show any sign of it as he released her hand.

"Your carriage is here," he said, nodding in the direction of the road. "Farewell, Cait."

"Goodbye," she replied, and watched as he turned abruptly and walked back inside. Then she took a deep breath and made her own way down the stairs.

CHAPTER EIGHT

Two days later, Cait bid farewell to a tearful mother and sister. She nearly had to pry Ginny's arms from around her waist to join her father in the hired carriage that would take her into the city. They had to take a longer route than they would normally have done. Unlike most of the young men who embarked on their National Service, Prince Felipe was getting a whole parade and many of the streets were closed. Her father helped her remove her things from the carriage and then they stood looking at each other, neither sure what to say.

"Be careful, Cait."

"I will."

"Don't get yourself hurt."

He held out a hand to her and she took it, and then moved in closer to embrace him. She had told herself that she wouldn't get emotional, but now that she was standing on the footpath with her things and about to be left to look after herself, it suddenly occurred to her exactly what she was doing. There was no backing out now, though, so she pulled away from her father, picked up her bag and made her way into the building.

Inside she met a group of other women who were also

going to be heading to the hospital with her that day. They were split up into four groups of three; these would be the groups they shared their dormitories with over their time there. Cait was teamed up with an older lady named Hattie and a younger, blonde girl named Meg. Hattie had worked at the farmer's market in the city, but her son had just been sent to the war and she wanted to be closer to him. Meg had grown up on a farm and said that this was the first time she was able to get away from five older brothers.

Hattie quirked an eyebrow at the younger girl when she heard this. "Don't go thinking this will be a glamorous job," she said. "It's not going to be fun."

"Oh, I know," Meg replied, "but at least I'll be doing something without being ordered about by older men."

Cait smiled. Meg was clearly a girl after her own heart.

Each woman there was issued with a uniform, including a pair of boots, three blouses with removable sleeves and a red cape. Cait thought the whole thing sounded impractical and wondered why they couldn't just wear the same clothes as the doctors they would be working alongside. She kept those thoughts to herself, though. Once they had everything, they were led to more coaches waiting out the back of the building. Their luggage was loaded and then they were helped into the carriages one at a time.

Once again, the most direct path was blocked because of the parade. Cait caught glimpses of the crowd lining the streets out the window of her carriage, but she didn't see anything of the prince himself. She wondered how he was feeling; no doubt he'd put on a good show while ever he was in the public eye, but once he was out of the spotlight, he might well have shown a different side of himself.

The journey to the Nardowyn-Gallit border was a long one, and they stopped for the night at an inn about two-thirds of the way there. Their coachman woke them early the next day and their journey continued. They arrived at the hospital around lunch time that day and were greeted by the Matron. The hospital was really one of the Royal Family's holiday houses, though it had been used less and less frequently in recent times, being so close to the Gallit border. It had been used as a hospital in the same fashion during the first war with Gallit, when King Gilles had still been a young prince, and he was happy to have it converted again when the second war began.

They were directed to the rooms that would be their dormitories. There were three beds, two against the walls, and one in the middle. There was just enough room in between each bed for a small bedside cupboard. The main building had three sprawling floors, while a separate wing at the back had always been used as the servants' quarters. That wing was now being used as accommodation for the nurses and as the mess hall, since the kitchen was already there.

In the main building, the ground floor was used for surgery and for those whose injuries were the most severe; the higher the floor number, the better the soldiers were doing. Makeshift "wards" had been created in different wings of the house and signs were written and stuck on the wall with pins to direct the nurses, doctors and more mobile patients.

Once Cait, Hattie and Meg had put their things in their dormitory, they joined the Matron and the other women who had arrived that day in the mess hall. The Matron ran them through the ground rules that they would be required to follow for the length of their stay. Each girl would receive two mornings or afternoons off a week, depending on their shifts. They would be learning on the job, since the need for new nurses was too great and there just weren't enough resources to train them beforehand. They had to be prepared to work night shifts as necessary, and to take on extra shifts at a moment's notice if they were required. Cait briefly wondered if she was really up to the task, but quickly told herself she was. It was no use getting cold feet now.

Once they had eaten lunch, Cait and her new colleagues were left to their own devices for the rest of the afternoon, though they were expected to be ready to work first thing the following morning. She, Hattie and Meg went back to their room and began to unpack. Cait was the first to finish; her roommates were still pottering around when she laid down on the bed she had claimed. She expected their movements to keep her awake, but they had travelled a fair distance and the bed at the inn the night before had been uncomfortable, so she found herself dozing off in spite of the noise surrounding her.

It was Hattie who woke her the following morning. At first, she tried rolling over, muttering that it was far too early to be getting up, but after a few moments she remembered where she was and sprang into wakefulness. When the three of them were ready, they made their way to the mess hall, where they had time to quickly gulp down a small breakfast, and then it was straight into the wards.

By the end of her first day shadowing some of the more experienced nurses, Cait had seen more blood pouring out of more wounds than she had ever seen in her life. She couldn't eat anything when she was granted half an hour for lunch; her appetite was long gone by then. Some of the soldiers' wounds had become infected and required cleaning or the application of special ointments - both things Cait would have rathered not do - but there was no choice in the matter. Sleep didn't come easily that night, but she told herself it would get easier. She only believed it a little.

Luckily, not every shift was spent in those wards, as she soon learned. Every few days, Cait was put to work upstairs with soldiers well on their way to recovery. It did not take her long to realise she much preferred this work to any other.

As she got to know them, she began asking the men in these wards about Prince Felipe, whether they had seen him at all and knew how he was doing. A couple of them had, one man named Angus and another called Samuel. According to them, the Prince had been automatically given the rank of captain, and was doing a fine job of leading his team of men. Very few of those under his command had suffered any injuries in the few weeks he had been with them.

To hear that he was performing so well brought a smile to Cait's face. She would freely admit that she had been worried about him. His anxiety leading up to leaving home had been obvious. She couldn't imagine the Prince Felipe she had come to know in those last few weeks being particularly keen on suddenly having a group of men looking up to him in the midst of conflict. She felt a little proud to hear that he was living up to expectations.

While it didn't stop her asking about him, Cait began to notice that a few of the other nurses were wondering why she was so interested in the Prince's movements. From what she heard mentioned in the mess hall and in the corridors, most people seemed to have heard that the Prince had often requested visits from a young woman from the city, but none of the other nurses seemed to know that Cait was the woman in question. Cait didn't

made any effort to make them aware of this fact. She was sure this was the best course of action, though it did mean that the other girls began to think that her questions indicated some strange fascination she had with him, like so many younger girls back in the city. She even heard it suggested that while some of the girls there might have been looking for a soldier husband, perhaps Cait was planning on seducing the Prince himself... despite him already being married. It seemed the girls who whispered like this were terribly worried that Cait would embarrass herself and everybody else dreadfully should the prince ever appear in their hospital. Cait let them whisper. She was fairly certain setting the record straight would not actually help.

As the weeks went on, Cait found that she did develop a stronger constitution for dealing with the injuries she had to face and treat, though she still preferred her shifts in the convalescent wards. She became good at knowing when to acknowledge a flirtatious remark from a bedridden soldier and when to ignore it. Though it took her longer, she also learned how to administer certain unpleasant medications or treatments without letting the moaning from the soldiers put her off.

It was towards the end of her second month in the hospital when Cait and her roommates were shaken awake by one of the nurses on the night shift. As they slowly came to, they could hear the rumblings of others who had already woken up and were hurriedly making their way towards the wards.

Cait had been on shift until after dinner, and pulled the blanket up over her head. "It's my day off," she mumbled, still half-asleep and not entirely coherent. "Leave me alone."

The blanket was deftly stripped away. "Don't be ridiculous," the nurse said tersely. "There's been an explosion and we've got dozens of men coming in. Including the Prince!".

CHAPTER NINE

Cait sat bolt upright. "Where is he?" she asked, grabbing the nurse's arm.

Recognising her, the nurse looked at Cait dubiously, and Cait was forced to remember how many of them thought she had a worrying obsession with Prince Felipe. She let go of the other woman's arm and got out of bed and began changing into her uniform.

"Where is he?" she asked again when she received no answer. The nurse told her, but then remarked none too quietly to the other two in the room that they ought to make sure Cait didn't do anything to embarrass herself.

Cait didn't give the others any time to stop her; they were still pulling on their boots when she left the room. Hattie called out her name but she ignored it and jogged up the path that led to the main building and down the hallway to where the nurse had told her she would find the prince.

When she reached it, she saw that extra stretcher beds had been set up and there were men on nearly every one of them. The stench of blood and mud hit Cait's nose as soon as she entered but by now she was used to blocking out that sort of thing and concentrating on the task at hand. She looked around, trying to spot the prince. He was nowhere in sight, but she did see a bed with four or five nurses, including the Matron, surrounding it. It stood to reason that paying so much attention to one patient was due to it being imperative to keep him alive.

Cait squeezed between beds and past nurses to reach his bedside. When she was closer, she could see his face; it was streaked with blood and sweat and his hair was caked with mud and goodness knew what else, but it was definitely Felipe. She elbowed her way past a nurse at his side, apologising but not really meaning it. When the other nurse realised who was pushing her out of the way, she exclaimed that Cait should not be involved there, and the Matron also began to tell Cait that it would be better if she left the Prince's welfare to the rest of them. Cait ignored them, taking one of the prince's hands in one of hers and pushing some of his hair out of his face with the other.

He was alternating between attempts at stoicism and raving from pain. A bandage covered a large section of his torso; one side of it was blood-soaked, indicating exactly where his wound was. Another bandage wrapped around half his left leg.

"Felipe?" she whispered, "Felipe, can you hear me?"

"Someone get her out of here," the Matron barked angrily, "Caitlin, control yourself! You don't have any right to —"

The Matron trailed off when she saw how Felipe's hands suddenly gripped Cait's and his eyes opened, recognition dawning as he focused his gaze on Cait's face. "Cait?"

"Yes, I'm here."

He tried to smile, but it came across as more of a wince. "And I'm not just dreaming?" he asked, his grip on her hand tightening.

"No," she said, squeezing his hand back, "you're not."

"Well, I know I'll be all right if I've got you."

Cait nodded, biting her lip. "You'll be fine."

"We need to get him to a doctor," the matron announced, "he is still losing blood." The other nurses began to move the stretcher out of the room, the matron held Cait back, giving her a curious look.

"I'm sure you're aware that your constant asking about the prince fired certain... rumours, and I'll admit to being a little concerned by some of the things I heard. I thought you were going to embarrass yourself and the rest of us if the prince was ever admitted here."

"I think a lot of people thought that, Matron."

The Matron nodded, acknowledging what Cait said, but leaving the topic be. "A lot of the girls talk about a woman that the prince would often invite to the palace. Was that you?"

"Yes, Matron."

"What was the purpose of those visits?"

"Conversation."

"And that was all?"

"Yes, Matron."

The Matron eyed Cait for a moment, not entirely believing her. "Very well," she finally said. "Off you go. Your services are needed."

"Of course."

While she worried about the prince for the rest of the night, Cait was kept busy seeing to other patients. Many of the men under Prince Felipe's command had been affected by the explosion. The Gallits had created an explosive that could be thrown into the camp, keeping them at some distance but scattering shrapnel down amongst the sleeping men on the other side of no man's land. Cait could not imagine what went on in the minds of the men who dreamed up such inventions.

Word came around the next afternoon that Prince Felipe had come through his surgery very well. The doctors had been able to remove the shrapnel from his side and most of it from his leg. However, the leg injury had been such that it would be some time before he would be able to walk properly again. The doctor had given him something to help him sleep and expected he would not wake until at least the evening. Cait had slept for most of the morning and was rostered on for the night shift again, so she visited him that afternoon, despite knowing she wouldn't be able to talk with him.

The mud and blood had been cleaned off his face and out of his hair and he had been dressed in clean, though very basic clothes. Had Cait not known who he was, it would have been very easy to mistake him for any one of the casualties who had come through the hospital in the time she had been there.

Despite what the doctor had given him, Felipe's sleep was not peaceful; he was frowning deeply and every now and then a murmured exclamation escaped his lips. Cait wanted to do something to soothe him, but didn't know what, so she simply laid a hand on his forehead, making gentle circular movements with her thumb. This seemed to have the desired effect, because his head stopped tossing and his outbursts quietened. Cait continued to do this for several minutes, until a voice behind her startled her into pulling her hand away.

"Word is, you're the prince's mistress and if his wife hadn't finally been able to conceive, they'd get you to do the job for her."

Cait turned around to come face-to-face with Doctor Brayden, one of the younger doctors in the hospital. She had met him a few times but had not had much to do with him. Due to her lack of training prior to her arrival at the hospital, Cait did not assist the doctors in surgery, and only saw them when they were doing their rounds in the wards.

At Doctor Brayden's words, she felt her cheeks darken, but she held his gaze steadily. "If that were the case, it would most certainly be none of your business, doctor. However, I can assure you and anyone else who chooses to talk behind my back like that, that my relationship with

Prince Felipe is nothing of that kind. I'll thank you not to speculate."

For a moment, Doctor Brayden looked as though he did not expect such a fiery reply, but then his expression became similar to the bemused one Prince Felipe used to wear when Cait argued with him during her early visits to the Palace. He didn't say anything, but turned and swanned out of the room with that same look on his face, as though enjoying some private joke.

Cait's cheeks were still burning, and after turning briefly back to Prince Felipe to ensure he was still sleeping peacefully, she marched out of the room and down to the Matron's office. She had no idea if the older woman would be in, or whether she would be busy attending patients or with other administration. It seemed luck was on Cait's side, however; when she knocked on the door, she heard the Matron's voice telling her to enter.

"You look upset, Caitlin," she said as Cait moved into the room. "Is everything all right?"

Cait sat down in the armchair on the other side of the Matron's desk. "Matron, I know what everyone says about Prince Felipe and me, and I know there's nothing I can do about it." The Matron nodded. "But even though I know what is being said, that doesn't mean I have to accept it when it is said to my face, does it?"

The Matron's eyes narrowed. "Who has spoken to you this way?" she asked.

"I went to see the prince this afternoon, even though I knew he would still be asleep. Doctor Brayden came into the room while I was there, and he told me everyone was saying that I was the prince's mistress, and that I would be used to bear an heir if Princess Maria had not been able to. I know what it must have looked like, me being summoned to the Palace every week, and trust me, I tried to tell the prince, but he is as stubborn as they come. I told Doctor Brayden that I did not appreciate him or anyone speculating like that, but I don't think he took any notice of me. That's why I came to you."

"Doctor Brayden will be spoken to, you have my word," Matron replied. "I will ensure he issues an apology to you, Caitlin."

Cait gave the Matron a small smile. "You can do that?" She hadn't been completely sure any of that would be in the Matron's power, but had not known where else she might turn. She didn't expect any of the other doctors would listen to her on the matter.

"Caitlin, I've been a nurse for over thirty years and a matron for ten of those. I think that gives me some sway."

Cait's smile became wider. "Thank you," she said, and stood up. "I'll return to my work now." She began to make her way towards the door but stopped when the Matron called her back.

"You are a good nurse, Caitlin," Matron said. "Don't let the rumours started by an ignorant few get to you."

Cait nodded. "I won't. Thank you."

CHAPTER TEN

For the next few days, it seemed that whenever Cait had free time, the Prince was asleep; whenever he was purportedly awake, she was on duty and couldn't get away.

Finally, however, Cait ducked her head into his room and found him sitting up in bed, a small tray hosting some food on his lap. When he saw her, his eyes lit up, and he quickly beckoned her into the room.

"I still can't believe you're here," he said to her as she sat down. "I mean, I know you told me you were coming, but..."

"I'm glad I came," Cait replied. "I almost wish I'd come sooner. They are so desperate for staff here."

"I still wish you didn't have to witness the effects of this war."

"I'll admit, it's nothing like Guy's letters made it out to be. He always sounded like he was having *fun*."

"They don't want anyone at home to know what it's like. They pretend it's all fun and games. Many of my own boys do exactly that when they write to their sweethearts back home."

"Your boys?" Cait couldn't help smiling at the affectionate term.

The Prince smiled sheepishly. "I suppose I've grown rather fond of them."

"I think it's sweet."

"You nearly left without telling me, didn't you? Our last afternoon together. We were already saying goodbye..."

"I didn't want you to try to talk me out of it," Cait replied.

"I'd certainly have tried my hardest."

"I know," said Cait, and batted him gently on one arm.

"Careful now," he warned her, grinning. "You don't want to be accused of assaulting the Crown Prince, do you?"

"Well, I'm already being accused of being your mistress, so it couldn't be that much worse."

"What do you mean?" The Prince's grin suddenly disappeared.

Cait shook her head. "It is exactly the same as the people back home. They find out we're meeting weekly and they make their own assumptions about it." She paused and wondered whether to continue. Deciding in the affirmative, she added, "And then some of them decide to mock me about it."

"Who? Tell me, Cait."

"Don't trouble yourself, it's been taken care of. You can't be getting upset about me while you are still recovering. If you're not careful, your doctor won't let me see you again until you're out of here."

"Cait... I know I have not put you in the best situation in these past few months. I might have been too stubborn to accept it whenever you pointed it out to me, but I want to make amends."

"What's done is done. I no longer blame you for it."

"Does that mean we're friends now, Cait?"

"We have been friends for some time now, Your Highness."

"Then you have no excuse to not call me Felipe." Cait

opened her mouth to object, but he held up a hand to silence her. "Please, Cait. You used my name when they first brought me in here and you held my hand in front of every other nurse who was on duty that night. You can use it when we are talking like this."

"All right... Felipe." She remembered she had used it that night, but she hardly thought that counted. She had just heard that he had been injured, probably badly, and she was not quite in her right mind. Calling him by his first name in normal conversation... it felt almost blasphemous.

They spoke for a few more minutes before Cait was forced to return to her duties for the afternoon. Prince Felipe put on a sulking expression as she stood to go, and with a roll of her eyes she promised she would come back the following day to talk, providing he was awake.

As it happened, though, she didn't even get as far as the wards the following morning; another nurse saw her in the hall on her way and told her the Matron wanted to see her. She assumed this was something to do with her complaint about Doctor Brayden; she had not heard anything further on that incident since it had occurred. She turned in the opposite direction and made her way back towards Matron's office.

Matron was writing when she entered the room and didn't immediately begin speaking. Cait sat down quietly in the other chair, folding her hands in her lap and waiting to be spoken to.

Finally, Matron looked up, placed down her pen and looked across the desk to Cait. "Thank you for coming, Caitlin. I believe that you have spoken to the Prince now?"

"Yes, Matron. I was able to see him briefly, yesterday."

"It must be a relief to you to see that he is recovering nicely."

"Yes, it is."

"When Doctor Raymond had finished examining the Prince yesterday, he suggested that it might be best that

His Highness have one nurse on duty for him around the clock. The Prince immediately requested you."

"Of course he did," Cait replied, her lips quirking.

Matron gave her a small smile in return and then continued, "On the one hand, I thought perhaps it would be ill-advised, when you are already the victim of so many rumours. However, I think perhaps the fact that you are already acquainted with him would make you the best choice. Would you be willing to accept this responsibility, Caitlin?"

"Of course."

"Then you will start immediately." Cait nodded and made to stand up but Matron waved her back down to her seat. "There was one other thing."

"Yes?"

"I have not forgotten the complaints you brought against Doctor Brayden. I went to speak to him myself and while he freely admits to speaking to you as you described, he does not seem to have any interest in making amends. Therefore, I will be speaking to his superiors as soon as opportunity allows me to."

"I don't want to cause any fuss," Cait said quietly.

"Nonsense!" the Matron exclaimed. "They cannot be allowed to think that they can get away with treating us as lesser beings. Our work here is just as important as theirs. Every now and then they are due for a reminder."

"If you are willing to go to these lengths for me, I am very grateful."

"It is no trouble. Now, off you go. I suggest you report to Doctor Raymond as soon as he is about. He will fill you in on the Prince's condition and what sort of care he will require."

"Of course. Thank you again, Matron."

Cait soon found out that Doctor Raymond had been on the previous night shift and would probably be sleeping until at least midday. Since she did not expect to see him until the afternoon, she returned to the wards to complete the shift she had originally been allotted. She alerted a few of the other girls to the fact that she was looking for the doctor and they agreed they would let her know should they see him.

In the end, it was the doctor who found Cait. Matron had seen him in the mess hall and had told him that Cait had agreed to take responsibility for the Prince. She joined him in the mess hall when her shift ended and found that he had covered an end of a table in notes on the Prince's condition, his injuries and how they should be treated.

While Doctor Raymond wanted to continue administering any pain-killing drugs himself and would continue to monitor the prince's progress, he was happy to allow Cait to administer sleeping medication if ever the Prince required it. Once the doctor was satisfied that Felipe was healed enough, Cait would also be needed on hand to assist with Felipe's exercising his injured leg, and eventually walking on it again.

"I must warn you, though," Doctor Raymond said when they had finished going through all the medical details, "he is already bored and complaining of a lack of fresh air in his room. In a few more days, it should be all right to move him. If I'm not to be found, ask some of the other doctors to help him into a wheelchair for you. A turn about the gardens might keep him quiet for a while."

Cait suppressed a smile. "Have no fear, Doctor," she said. "I think I am quite capable of handling the Prince's whining."

"Good girl. Well, that is all you need to hear from me. You may start these new duties immediately. I'll tell Matron to find someone else to cover your regular shifts on the current roster."

"Thank you, Doctor." Cait gathered up the supplies he had provided her with and then made her way back to the private room where the Prince was to be found.

"Well, I hear you're causing trouble already," she said by way of greeting.

"How so?" Felipe's brow furrowed. The comment genuinely confused him.

"Doctor Raymond did not seem too pleased that he has to put up with your complaints about your accommodation."

The Prince frowned. "I can't tell them the real reason it bothers me so much," he said quietly.

"What do you mean?"

"I'm sure you're aware that this house belongs to my family. This was Sebastian's room whenever we stayed here."

"Oh…"

"Everything in here reminds me of him."

"Felipe, I'm sorry. But I don't know that there will be anywhere to move you. We're so pressed for space as it is."

"If it's at all possible, Cait. I would give anything to get out of here."

"I'll see what I can do. In the meantime, Doctor Raymond seems to think we'll be able to move you in a few days. Then we can put you in a wheelchair - don't look at me like that, you can't walk just yet - but we can take you outside."

Felipe's sigh of relief was audible. "Well, better than nothing," he conceded. "There's something I wanted to ask you," he continued, his expression becoming serious again. "I hadn't been game enough to ask before but I think I can cope with you giving me the news. How many of my men survived?"

"I wouldn't know one of your men from any other soldier here. I would have to ask one of the registrars, or you would have to give me a list of names you would like investigated."

"I can do that. Can you get me a pen and paper?" He seemed to be sitting up straighter with keenness.

"Don't excite yourself," Cait reprimanded him gently, patting him on the shoulder to indicate he should relax back into his pillows. "I will go and fetch you some."

The walk down to the stores took Cait several minutes, and while pen and paper were easy enough to find, she had to hunt around for a bottle of ink. When she finally returned to the Prince's room, she found two men fitting out the room next to it with a small cot and a bedside chest, which would be for her use. It hadn't occurred to her that she would be expected to spend her nights near Prince Felipe as well, but then she remembered Matron had referred to her new duties as "around the clock care" so of course it made sense. How else would she know when she would need to administer the sleeping medication to the prince?

She delivered the pen, ink and paper to Felipe, setting the tray that was usually for his food over his bed so he had something to lean on. While he was occupied with writing the list of names, she went to retrieve a few of her things from her dormitory. When she got there, she found Hattie lying on the bed, reading.

"Where are you off to?" she asked Cait, looking up curiously as Cait began picking up her clothes and placing them in a bag. "You're not leaving us halfway through the rotation, are you?"

"Not exactly," Cait replied, and then explained the day's events.

"Why did you never tell us you were the Prince's friend?" Hattie asked. "I'll admit, even Meg and I thought it a bit strange the way you were always asking about him."

"I became quite used to rumours about me spreading," Cait replied, "and besides, most people wouldn't have believed me had I said that mine and the prince's meetings were simply borne out of friendship."

"I would have!" Hattie exclaimed, sounding affronted, "and I'm sure Meg would have as well!"

Cait smiled over her shoulder at the other woman. "Well, you know now. We'll still see each other in the mess halls and in the wards every now and then, won't we?"

"I'll make sure of it. Good luck, Cait."

"Thank you, Hattie." Giving her friend another smile, Cait picked up the bag of possessions she had packed and headed back to her new bedroom. She dropped her things on her bed, pocketed the room key that had been left on the dresser with a short note of explanation, and returned next door to see how the prince had progressed with his list.

He had written down the names of about fifteen men to whom he had been close. Cait took the piece of paper and promised to take it to the registrar first thing in the morning. It was getting towards evening and it was likely that the registration office would be unattended by now.

There was little else for Cait to do for the evening. Doctor Raymond arrived at around eight o'clock, accompanied by a kitchen hand with food for both Cait and Felipe. Once they had eaten, the doctor checked over Felipe's injuries and changed the dressings with Cait's assistance.

"I am repulsed every time he takes the bandages off me," Felipe remarked when the doctor had left, "but you didn't even bat an eyelid, Cait. How do you do it?"

"I had to get used to blood and worse things very quickly once I arrived here," Cait replied. "You learn to ignore it after a while."

"You are a better person than I, Cait."

It was later that night that Cait discovered why Doctor Raymond had wanted her on hand to administer sleeping draughts. The wall between her room and Felipe's was only thin, and in his sleep, he was crying out loud enough to wake her.

She lit a candle and hurriedly pulled a coat on over her nightdress to avoid having to dress properly, then darted out of her own room and into the Prince's. He had tossed off half the bedclothes and had become entangled in the sheets, which to Cait just made his helpless thrashing on the bed seem all the more heartbreaking.

She quickly crossed to the bedside and tried to get a firm grasp on Felipe's arms to hold him still. Usually, when a patient was suffering from nightmares such as these, Cait would have the assistance of one of the other nurses, but on her own, it was difficult to prevent the prince from moving; he was much stronger than she.

"Felipe!" she called a few times, raising her voice above his own cries. "Felipe, you must wake up! You're dreaming; please wake up!"

It took a few minutes, but finally the Prince's eyes flew open and he gasped. He fought to control his breathing (which was coming in short bursts) and looked around the room wildly until his eyes fixed on Cait in the candlelight. One of his hands unconsciously reached for hers where it still held onto his forearm.

"Cait?" His voice was uncertain.

"I'm here," she assured him, wiping his hair from his sweat-soaked forehead with her free hand. "You're safe now."

"I was dreaming?"

"Yes."

"I don't think I ever want to dream again. This war... it will be in my head forever. And I haven't even been here as long as some."

"Doctor Raymond has shown me the medicine to help you sleep. Would you like some?"

"Will it help? Surely then I will be trapped in whatever nightmares plague me."

Cait hadn't thought of that. "I don't know," she admitted, "but you can hardly go through life refusing to ever sleep again."

"That is true. If I take the medicine, will you stay with me until you are sure the dreams have not come again?"

"If that is what you would prefer."

"It is."

"Very well." Cait paused and smiled slightly before adding, "you are going to have to let go of my hand if I am to go and fetch it."

It seemed that this was the first inkling Felipe had that he had been holding her hand at all, and he looked down at his fingers covering hers with some surprise. Now that he was aware of it, he seemed reluctant to let go, but eventually he lowered his hand.

Cait quickly ducked back to her room to retrieve the medicine. She poured the correct amount into a medicine glass on her way back and handed it to Felipe when she reached his bedside again. Before he drank it, he looked up at Cait, who had pulled a chair closer to the bed and sat down. In that moment, Cait thought he looked about half his age, a lost little boy.

"You will stay, won't you?" he asked quietly.

"Of course I will. You have nothing to worry about."

Felipe looked away, staring into the medicine the way a drunk might stare into the bottom of his glass. "It's awful, you know," he said, "feeling this powerless. I can't just send someone else to deal with my dreams the way I would for anything else."

"Perhaps once you are more mobile you could spend some time in the convalescent wards. It might not make the nightmares go away, but many of the men in there would understand what you are going through. It might do you good to talk to them."

Felipe nodded and said, "Yes, I think I'd like that," before downing the medicine and handing the glass back to Cait. He settled down into his pillows and Cait sat quietly next to him until his eyes drooped closed. Once his breathing evened out and she was sure he was asleep, she allowed another hour to see if the nightmares returned. When he was still sleeping soundly after that time, she slipped out of the room and back to her own bed.

Felipe slept soundly the rest of that night. So began a routine wherein Cait kept him company when he took the medicine before settling down to sleep, and only left when she was sure he would not wake up. This plan did not work perfectly, but for the most part, her company seemed to soothe him.

As Doctor Raymond had predicted, a few days later it was declared the Felipe was able to be moved should he so desire. The Prince looked as though the only reason he was not jumping for joy was that in his current state he could not do so without doing more damage to himself. A wheelchair was brought from one of the wards and two of the younger doctors helped lift Felipe into it, and then carefully carried him down the stairs to the main door. As they returned to their regular duties, they told Cait to let them know when she needed them to help return the prince to his room.

As she wheeled him past one of the wards on the way out to the gardens, he asked, "Cait, how many proposals of marriage have you received since you've been here?"

"I beg your pardon?"

"I know what these men would be like, Cait. You're a pretty woman and they don't see *any* women, pretty or otherwise, until they end up here."

Cait laughed. "To date, I have received no marriage proposals," she informed him, "but the outrageously flirtatious remarks already number in the thousands, I expect."

Felipe laughed at this, but then cringed and placed a hand on the wound on his side. "Well, I'd be disappointed to hear anything less," he said.

"Are you all right?" Cait asked, her smile disappearing and concern taking its place. Judging by the expression on the prince's face, the wound was still smarting.

"I'm fine," he said through clenched teeth. "I just have to remember to remain completely serious at all times until this damn thing is healed." He paused and glanced up at Cait, and then added, "Please forgive my language."

"I've heard a lot worse in my time here."

By this time they had reached the gardens and Cait manoeuvred the prince's chair next to a bench where she

85

could sit down herself. She and some of the other nurses often brought their patients from the convalescent wards to this spot. Under other circumstances, it might have been considered romantic, but to the soldiers it was simply a respite from the sights, sounds and smells of the wards.

"Do you have a favourite patient?" Felipe asked.

"Not really. They come and go so quickly," Cait replied. "You think you're getting to know them and becoming their friend and then suddenly they're gone. Either they're discharged and sent back to the front or..." She trailed off, but Felipe understood exactly what she wasn't saying.

They moved onto other subjects quickly and the rest of the afternoon was spent in much more pleasant conversation.

Felipe had received a letter from Princess Maria, updating him on daily life back at the palace. She was now about six months along, and feeling the baby moving more regularly.

A subconscious smile spread across Felipe's face as he told Cait of this, causing her to smile as well. It seemed that in spite of the apprehension he had seemed to be showing about his impending fatherhood the day he and Cait had spoken in the funerary grove, it seemed the prospect of becoming a father excited him as well.

CHAPTER ELEVEN

It was as Cait was returning the Prince to his room that afternoon that she heard Doctor Brayden's voice behind her. "Caitlin, may I have a word?"

At first, Cait was inclined to respond that she was busy and request he come back later. However, the two younger doctors who had helped her with the prince earlier had returned to help him back to his room, and she knew that she could spare the few minutes. Whatever Doctor Brayden had to say to her (and it didn't sound like he had come to apologise), it would be better to get it out of the way than prolong the wait.

"You go ahead," she said to the prince and the other doctors, and then turned to Doctor Brayden. "Yes, Doctor? What is it?"

"I've been advised that I should apologise for the way I spoke to you, though I cannot believe such a fuss has been made over one harmless remark."

"It may have seemed harmless to you, Doctor, but you do not have to live with such comments on a regular basis. I assure you, they pile up."

The doctor's face twitched slightly; it was clear that he was not used to apologising for his words. "Then I am sorry, Caitlin, if my comments offended you at all."

Cait bristled at the conditional apology, but all she said was, "Thank you, Doctor. I appreciate that."

"You're welcome," he replied, turning to leave. "Though next time, I would thank you to not go complaining straight to my superiors."

"Oh, I didn't," Cait replied innocently. "I only spoke to Matron. *She* went to your superiors. Most people here realise that the nurses deserve as much respect as you; perhaps you should do the same."

Doctor Brayden only glared again, and turned on his heel and marched away. Cait wondered if she had got the last word over the doctor, but she wasn't feeling particularly victorious as she made her way down the corridor towards the prince's room.

"Who was that?" Felipe asked as she sat down by his bed.

"Doctor Brayden," Cait replied. "He came to apologise for... for a misunderstanding we had recently."

"A misunderstanding?"

"Well... he was the one who said I was your mistress."

Felipe frowned. "You call that a misunderstanding?"

"I didn't want you to overreact."

"You said that it had been taken care of."

"It had."

"The why was he only apologising to you now?"

"Look, there are processes in place for this sort of thing. I went through all the proper channels and now it *has* been taken care of. Please don't make this any bigger than it needs to be. I don't need you to be outraged on my behalf."

The prince took a deep breath, and then nodded. "You're right. I'm sorry, Cait."

The following morning, Cait received a message that the registrar had completed his checking of Felipe's list. It was with some trepidation that she approached his office. She had seen the devastation of the explosion that had injured Felipe; his men would have had to have been very lucky to all come out of it alive.

The registrar confirmed her fears as he handed back the list along with a few extra pages. "I don't envy you bringing the news to him," he said.

"I wish I didn't have to," Cait replied, "but the sooner, the better, I suppose. Were you able to find a room he might be moved to?"

"I'm afraid not. The only available ones are too small, about the size of your room. He would need one a wheelchair can be taken into, and you need room to move around in there."

"That's all right. Thank you for trying."

She made her way to Felipe's room and stood outside for a few minutes, preparing herself for how she expected he would receive the news of the fate of so many of his men. She took a deep breath and then knocked on the door. Felipe's voice came from within, inviting her inside.

Felipe had not long finished breakfast and the little table that fit across the bed was still in front of him, an empty plate and mug sitting on it. She had barely entered the room when he saw the paper in her hand and correctly guessed what it was.

"Is it good news or bad?" he asked as Cait sat down.

"A bit of both," Cait replied. "Do you want me to read it to you or do you want to read it yourself?"

"I'll read it."

Cait handed him the papers from the registrar and then watched him closely as he read. The further he got, the more his brow furrowed, until his expression was darker than Cait had ever seen it.

When he finished, he lowered the papers slowly, but he didn't look at Cait. He just stared at the wall instead. Cait didn't know whether to try to say something comforting or to let him process everything in silence.

A few minutes later, when he had still barely moved, she leaned forward and placed a hand on the edge of his bed. "Felipe?"

He turned in her direction, but barely seemed to register she was there. "So many of them are dead," he said. "Why should I have survived when they did not?"

"That is what happens in war."

This didn't placate him at all. "Look," he said, motioning to one of the names on the list. The registrar had written "Died of wounds" next to it. "This man had a wife."

"So do you."

Felipe managed to raise an eyebrow at Cait without any of the wit or humour Cait had come to associate with that expression.

"His wife was his entire world. He never stopped talking about her. You of all people should know, Cait, that I can only wish for a love like that." Cait didn't respond. "*These* men deserved to live far more than I. But, no, it's all 'Quick, we have to save the Prince. The Prince must be saved!'" Cait had never heard him sound so bitter about his position in life.

"Please, Felipe, don't talk like that."

"WELL, IT'S TRUE!"

As he yelled the words, he slammed his fist down on the breakfast tray, causing the plate and mug to rattle. Cait winced and sat back in her seat, deciding Felipe needed the space.

After a few deep breaths, he turned to look at Cait and his expression softened. "I'm sorry, Cait. I shouldn't be taking this out on you. I thought I'd prepared myself for this but... seeing it written, I just..." He trailed off and looked away, tight-lipped. It was clear to Cait he was struggling to maintain his composure.

"Should I go?" she asked quietly.

"No, please stay. I won't lose my temper again. I don't want to be alone, Cait."

"All right."

Not much was spoken between them for the rest of the

morning and it wasn't until lunchtime that Cait felt she could bring up the subject of Felipe's men again.

"I don't know if you noticed, but some of your men who survived are also patients here. I could see if they're mobile if you like... They could come and see you, or once you're up and about, you could see them."

"Yes," Felipe nodded. "Not for a few days, though. I don't know if I could face any of them just yet."

"Of course. Just let me know and I'll see what I can do."

Once Felipe had eaten lunch that day, Cait helped him to sit up with his legs over the side of the bed.

"Doctor Raymond wants me to see how much mobility there is in your injured leg," she said. "We might be able to have you walking soon. Can you lift it?"

She watched closely as Prince Felipe raised his left leg slowly, and bent it at the knee. He tried to hide the grimace as it hurt him towards the end, but Cait's eye was astute enough to see it.

"Don't force it," she told him firmly. "The last thing we want is for it to be damaged further."

"I want to walk again, Cait," Felipe replied. "I'm so sick of having to be wheeled around. Of relying on everyone else!"

"I know," Cait replied. "But this isn't something that can be rushed."

Cait spent the next little while continuing her assessment of Felipe's leg. She tested the range of movement in a few different ways, comparing it with his uninjured leg. As far as she could tell, the external wound was healing well, but she wasn't sure if his leg as a whole would be strong enough to bear weight just yet.

When she finished her examination, she could tell Felipe was worried she was going to tell him it would still be some time before he was allowed to attempt to walk again. Instead of disappointing him, she said she would talk to Doctor Raymond and discuss with him how to move forward.

"You're just trying to let me down easily," Felipe complained.

"I am not. Maybe Doctor Raymond will surprise us."

That afternoon, she took Felipe outside as normal, and they ran into Hattie, who was also outside with a few other nurses and their patients. At first, none of them seemed to know how to act in the presence of the Crown Prince, but Cait began introducing him to the people she knew, hoping she might be able to encourage some of the other men to talk with him. The men all introduced themselves by rank and battalion, and Felipe was familiar with some of the actions they had taken part in. Once that was established, the other men seemed to accept Felipe as one of their group, and the conversation began to flow.

Cait, Hattie and the other nurses moved away a little. Their patients often thought they ought to censor themselves in front of the nurses, and it seemed to be beneficial for the men if the nurses kept an eye on them from a distance and let them talk amongst themselves.

"How is the Prince recovering?" Hattie asked.

"Pretty well," Cait replied. "He's getting restless, though. I'm hoping Doctor Raymond says he'll be able to try walking soon."

"I heard the wound in his leg was the worse of the two."

"I think so. The one on his side was painful for him but fairly shallow. The leg is worse. He's lucky it didn't shatter his knee."

When Cait returned Felipe to his room later that afternoon, there was a broad smile on his face. He didn't share much of what he had talked about with the other men, but it had clearly done him some good. After that, she organised a few more gatherings with the other nurses. Not all of them resulted in the same smile as the first one; sometimes Felipe would return to his room in pensive silence, causing Cait to wonder what would cause him to draw into himself like that.

A few days later, Cait found time to report to Doctor Raymond on the condition of Felipe's leg. Doctor Raymond noted Cait's concerns, but decided that perhaps it was time for Felipe to attempt putting weight on the injured leg and begin exercising it that way. Even if it were only for a few minutes a day, it would at least give the prince the psychological benefit of feeling like he was beginning to make some progress.

The following day, Cait went outside on her own to clear the area and ensure they could be alone. Doctor Raymond appeared soon after, wheeling Felipe. Before he let Felipe out of the wheelchair, Doctor Raymond insisted on some simple exercises to warm his leg up and work out some of the stiffness that would probably plague it at first. Once he was satisfied with that, he moved several paces away before turning and looking at Cait and Felipe expectantly.

Cait put her hands under Felipe's arms and helped him to stand. He leaned on her heavily. "Are you all right?" she asked.

"Fine," he replied, though it did not sound convincing. She could feel him shaking, and trying to put as much weight as possible onto his uninjured leg.

"All right," she said. "One step at a time."

Slowly, Felipe extended his left leg and then put it on the ground in front of him. He transferred his weight to it, and then very quickly took another step to relieve its burden.

"That's it," Cait encouraged.

He took another couple of steps, still favouring his uninjured leg, but gaining more confidence. He began to lean on Cait a little less as he took another step, and that was when he stumbled as his leg buckled underneath him. Cait was still holding onto him and managed to slow his fall; as soon as he was on the ground she turned to retrieve the wheelchair.

Felipe cursed loudly, but then looked apologetically at Cait as she helped him up. She placed a comforting hand on his shoulder. She knew he wasn't going to take too kindly to simply being told that it would take some time for him to get back on his feet.

"Not to worry, Your Highness," Doctor Raymond said. "We'll get you there." He joined them and patted the prince on the other shoulder. He retracted it quickly when Felipe glared at him.

"I have had enough of this for today," Felipe said. "You may go, Doctor."

Doctor Raymond looked a little taken aback at the abrupt dismissal, but he nodded. "Of course, Your Highness. Perhaps we can try again tomorrow." He bowed his head slightly and then quickly made his way back towards the hospital building.

"That wasn't nice, you know," Cait chided Felipe when Doctor Raymond was out of earshot.

"I don't care," Felipe grumbled, glowering down at his knees.

"You have to have patience."

"I am sick of hearing that!"

Cait didn't respond and Felipe lowered his voice. "Please, can we go back inside, Cait?"

Cait nodded and began wheeling the chair back inside. Once the prince was settled back in his room, she left him alone for the rest of the evening. His mood hadn't improved much, and she thought he was probably best left to his own thoughts.

CHAPTER TWELVE

For several days after that, Doctor Raymond joined Cait and Felipe at some point during the day, and Felipe attempted to walk the few steps from his bed or wheelchair to where the doctor stood. He still relied heavily on Cait's support, but slowly he progressed from dragging his bad leg along the ground to taking hesitant steps. Another week and he was able to simply hold onto Cait's arm, rather than cling to her entire body. He still limped, and the movement in his leg was limited, but it was nonetheless a decided improvement. Doctor Raymond found him a walking stick so that he could get about on his own and when it was clear he was going to continue improving, Cait was gradually reinstated into the regular duties that she had been performing in the wards before Felipe's arrival.

Her bed in the dormitory had been kept free in anticipation of her return. Both Meg and Hattie were working when Cait arrived back there with her things; when they returned that night, Meg let out a squeal of delight and hugged Cait tightly. Hattie displayed her pleasure at Cait's return a little less enthusiastically, but with no less warmth. That night the three of them stayed up longer than they probably should have, sharing gossip they had picked up from around the wards and talking about various patients.

Cait still visited Prince Felipe whenever she had a chance, and regaled him with stories from her new patients. Every now and then she would mention the flirting she was often on the receiving end of. She would giggle when Felipe bristled with indignation on her behalf, and remind him that not long after he had arrived, he had said he expected nothing less than that behaviour. On one or two occasions, he then went on to ask about Doctor Brayden; Cait assured him that she had barely seen the doctor since their disagreement, and told Felipe he had nothing to worry about.

A couple of weeks after she returned to regular duties, Cait's dinner was interrupted by none other than Felipe, who had come to find her in the mess hall. He was leaning on his walking stick, and there was sweat on his forehead. He hadn't yet walked any kind of distance such as that from his room to the mess.

"What are you doing here!" Cait exclaimed. "You shouldn't -"

"I need to talk to you. Somewhere private."

His expression was so determined that Cait found herself standing up to go with him. She heard a few of the nurses making comments as she left the hall with him, but she was well used to ignoring them by this point. She followed Felipe as he strode from the smaller building to the edge of the gardens. The sun was beginning to set but there was still enough light for them to see where they were going. Cait noticed that he was relying on his cane more than he had been recently. Was something bothering him enough to cause it?

Finally he stopped and turned to face Cait.

"What's wrong?" she asked.

"I received a letter from home today," he said, pulling

the letter in question out of a pocket in his trousers. His tone suggested that it did not contain good news.

"Yes?"

"The baby came early," he said, turning away from Cait and pacing down the path along the edge of the garden. After a few strides he stopped, turned and made his way back. "That on its own would not be a problem. But there were complications." He paced away from Cait again.

"What complications?" she asked quietly. She had a feeling she already knew.

Felipe turned around again. "Maria did not survive," he said abruptly.

Cait felt her heart sink. She moved towards him and took his free hand. He gripped it tightly.

"Are you all right?" she asked gently.

"I..." For the first time since he had found her in the mess hall, Felipe became less restless. "I don't feel anything. Is that terrible?"

"It is a shock for you."

"No, it's not that." Felipe turned so he was not quite facing Cait. "It's more... well, I'm expected to mourn for my wife, yes? But I barely knew her. We shared a bed at night, but little else. My immediate reaction is to be daunted by the prospect of having to pretend to feel more than I do... than to actually feel anything." Cait nodded. What he said made sense, but she didn't know what to say in response. "There's another thing as well," he continued after a while. "The child is a girl. I still don't have an heir, so I doubt my father will let me return to the front. He learned that lesson with Sebastian. Maria's funeral has been delayed to allow me time to return home for it. I don't expect I'll be back."

"When are you leaving?"

"Early tomorrow. It has all been arranged."

"So this is the last I'll see of you, I suppose."

"Yes." Silence fell between them until Felipe asked, "Cait, how much longer are you here for?"

"I've still got a few months on my rotation."

Felipe turned and faced Cait properly. He was still holding her hand and he held it up between them, clasping it tightly. "Cait, when you come home, will you marry me?"

Cait took a step back and pulled her hand away. "Mother Above, Felipe, your wife has just died," she said. "How can you ask me that?"

"I'm not suggesting it happen next week. You can finish here and then it could be announced once you came home. Enough time will have passed by then."

"You don't know what you're saying."

"What do you want me to say, Cait? Yes, my wife has died and yes, I am saddened that my daughter will never know her mother, but I only married Maria because I could tell even on that night we met that you would have refused me. I even said so, remember? I let you go because I could tell at the time that you only had eyes for Guy. That was obvious, even without ever seeing the two of you together. But it's always been you, have you never realised that?"

"I would have refused you? I doubt your father would have ever let you ask me!"

"Either way, Cait! I am not going to mourn a woman I barely had anything to do with when the woman I love is standing right in front of me!"

Cait did not reply, but took another step back and stared at Felipe, trying to process everything he had just said. Her heart had leapt quite involuntarily at his pronouncement, but her head told her that he was grieving, even if he claimed he wasn't, and in shock, too. Surely he didn't know what he was saying.

To fill in the silence that was stretching out between the two of them, Felipe continued, "Tell me you do not feel the same and I will never mention the subject again. But you said yourself you came here to 'keep your eye on me'. I know of very few respectable women who would do that for their husband or even their brother, so tell me, Cait, what am I supposed to take from that?"

Cait did not know what to say. She wished she was rostered on that night so that she could make hurried excuses and run to her work. Her cheeks were burning and her head was pounding, which made it difficult to concentrate on forming a solid reply.

"I have to go," she said finally, and turned on her heel and ran back towards her dormitory, leaving Prince Felipe in her wake.

CHAPTER THIRTEEN

"Cait, are you all right?"

Meg and Hattie came off shift together later that night and they found Cait sitting on her bed with her knees pulled up to her chest. She looked like she had been crying but now she was just staring at the opposite wall.

"Cait?" Meg tried again.

Hattie sat down on the bed next to Cait. "What's wrong, love? Was it something the Prince said to you tonight?"

Cait looked at her sharply. "You weren't there," she said. "How did you -"

"It's not very often there's a prince in the mess hall," Hattie said. "Word got around."

Cait rolled her eyes. "Of course it did," she muttered. "It always does."

"Now what's the matter?" Hattie pressed. "Did he hurt you? Offend you somehow?"

Cait turned her head to focus on Hattie. "He told me his wife had died," she said. "And then he asked me to marry him."

Cait saw the eyes of both women widen. Meg came and sat on the middle bed, facing them.

"The death of his wife aside," Hattie said, "I take it that's not what you wanted?"

"How can he be thinking of marrying me before she is even cold in her grave? He says he doesn't mourn her, that he barely knew her and that -" Cait paused and took a deep breath - "and that he has always loved me, but... I don't know if I can believe it."

"Why not?" Meg replied. "It's no secret that he and Princess Maria weren't close. He's always been much more fond of you."

"Has he? How well do you know him?"

"I..." Meg trailed off and sat back a little, avoiding Cait's gaze.

"I think the other question we need to be asking," Hattie said, drawing them back to the issue at hand, "is do you love him?"

"I... I'm scared, Hattie," Cait replied, her voice very quiet. "I'm not prepared for that sort of life! It was all right before; he was married, so there was no possibility... but now..."

In response, Hattie just held her close for a few moments, and then stood up, taking Cait by the shoulders. "Best thing for you now is to get some sleep. You'll feel better in the morning."

Cait didn't think she would sleep at all, but she accepted her nightgown when Hattie passed it to her and settled down under her blankets. She was surprised how easily she ended up dozing off.

By the time Cait had a free moment the following day, Prince Felipe was already gone. A part of her had hoped the he might have tried to find her to say goodbye before he left, but after their argument, it didn't really surprise her that he took off without another word to her.

She carried on with her work and tried not to think about him. She was grateful when Hattie and the others made attempts to cheer her up, even if they weren't always successful. During her time off, however, all she could hear in her head was Prince Felipe's voice telling her he loved her, followed by feeling like her stomach had just plummeted to the floor, just as she felt the first time she heard the words.

"I just wish he hadn't taken me by surprise!" she ranted to Hattie and Meg one night when the three of them were all off-shift. "And I wish I hadn't just run away. I just want it to all be resolved, but who knows when that will happen." She looked up at her roommates fearfully. "I don't even know if he'll want to see me again."

"Cait," Hattie said calmly, moving from her bed to Cait's and putting an arm around Cait's shoulder. "If he loves you as he said he did, a silly argument isn't going to change that. He'll see you again."

"I don't know," Cait argued. "He can be stubborn when he wants to be."

"Cait, you have to stop thinking about the worst that could happen. Have some hope. Anyway, it's time you were out of here. You're going to be late."

Cait and Meg were rostered on the late shift that night, and Hattie was right. They were running late. Thankfully, their rounds were fairly routine. There were no new admissions in the ward they were in, and most of the men were sleeping. Only a few needed late-night doses of their medication.

They had been working for a couple of hours when they heard the first round of gunfire. Many of the men immediately sprang awake, several with gasps or loud cries. The shots had come from outside and had scared the nurses as much as the patients, but they did their best to keep the men calm. In some cases, this was easier said than done, particularly as more shots were fired soon after and at least some of those seemed to come from inside the building.

They could hear gruff voices yelling from downstairs and then heavy footsteps beginning to run down the corridors. Closer by, patients were also starting to yell, wanting to know where the noise was coming from. Meg grabbed Cait's arm and tugged her out of the ward and onto the balcony that looked over the ground floor. From there they could see several men in black uniforms, and their yelling became clearer; those were definitely Gallit accents Cait could hear.

"What are they doing here?" Meg exclaimed.

"Prince Felipe," Cait said, suddenly realising. "Somehow they found out he was here, and they don't know that he's left."

"Then we have to let them know!"

Meg tugged on Cait's arm to pull her down the stairs, but Cait pulled her back. "You stay up here," she said. "I'll go."

"I'm not letting you go alone!" Meg replied.

"You're too -"

"Don't tell me I'm too young, Cait! There are only two years between us and if this hospital is overrun by Gallit forces, I'm going to be in just as much danger as anyone else."

"All right, then, come on!"

Together they ran down the elaborate staircase that took up most of the entrance hall. By the time they reached the ground floor, several of their colleagues were running in different directions. Men's voices, belonging to both Gallit invader and Nardowyn patient, were echoing through the corridors, making it almost impossible to make out what anyone was actually saying.

There was a Gallit soldier coming towards Meg and Cait, though he altered his course slightly to veer around them. Cait stuck out a hand and grabbed a handful of his sleeve, forcing him to stop. He wrenched himself out of Cait's grasp and turned to face her with a growl.

"What is your business here?" she asked. "Are you looking for Prince Felipe?"

"Aye," the Gallit man said, looking at Cait suspiciously. "Tell us where he is and we can be on our way sooner."

"You've missed him by over a week. His wife passed away and he returned home for her funeral last Saturday."

"Oh, well, that is sad. You seem to know his movements well. Are you the girl who looked after him?" Cait's silence seemed to answer the question for him. "Apparently His Royal Highness is quite keen on you."

Cait and Meg shared a look. Who had told them about Cait's relationship with the Prince? There was no time for dwelling too much, though, since the two men were advancing upon them now.

"Perhaps if we take you, the Prince'll come looking and be led straight to us."

"What?" Of all the scenarios that had flashed through Cait's head in the moments before she and Meg had come downstairs, this was not one of them. She had not expected to be recognised, nor for the men to want anything more to do with her than any of the other women.

"Cait, I think we should go." Meg grasped Cait's upper arm and tugged her back towards the stairs. Cait, however, found that being in real danger for the first time since leaving home had rooted her to the spot.

"Cait!" Meg's voice was urgent, but she didn't wait for Cait to follow her. As the Gallit man reached out for Cait, Meg let go of her and ducked away. The loss of contact jolted Cait into action but by then it was too late. As she turned to follow, the Gallit man grabbed her by the arm and pulled her roughly towards him. She stumbled and he was able to grab her other arm as well, pinning them behind her back. Cait tried to struggle, but his grip was far too tight for her to break, and she had no choice but to go where he pushed her.

When Cait was pushed through the door, it was dark, but the Gallit men had enough lanterns for her to be able to see several riderless horses and a wagon waiting in the entrance area to the hospital compound. When the man holding Cait prisoner explained to his comrades who Cait was, many of them expressed delight at seeing her.

"Well, the Prince'll be out here as quick as he can when he knows we've got you," one said smugly.

"Yes, if we couldn't find him, you're the next best thing," agreed another.

"How do you know about my friendship with the prince?" Cait asked, once again struggling against the grip of the man who was pinning her arms to her side. "Who told you?"

"Friendship, is that what they're calling it now?" said the smug man, and they all roared with laughter. Cait felt her cheeks turn red.

"Don't ask questions you don't want answered," the man holding her muttered loudly in her ear, prompting more laughter.

This only made Cait more curious, in spite of her current circumstances. "Who told you?" she pressed.

"I'm sure you'll find out soon enough," she was assured.

"You think this is a good idea, but you're wrong," she said, feeling braver; arguing with men who talked down to her was familiar territory. "If the Prince was to come to find me himself, which I doubt, do you think he'd come alone?"

"We're well-prepared," said a tall man who exited the hospital in time to hear Cait's question. He came toward Cait and examined her closely. "You're a pretty thing. I can see why he likes you."

"As far as I know, my looks have nothing to do with it."

The man cocked his head at her. "Cheeky, too." He looked over Cait's head at the man holding her. "Put her in the wagon. We'll take her with us."

The man holding Cait said, "Yes, sir," and pushed Cait along in front of him towards a wagon with two horses hitched at the front. Another man opened the doors at the back and Cait was unceremoniously pushed up the stairs and inside. Her foot caught on the top step and she tripped, thrusting her hands out in front of her to break her fall. This resulted in grazes on both her hands, and she expected there would be bruises on her legs as well.

The wagon door was slammed shut behind her, and she heard it lock on the outside. There were no windows and nothing to sit on or make the journey more comfortable. She didn't know where the men planned on taking her, but she sat in one corner and tucked her knees under her chin. If luck would have it, the journey would only be a short one.

Once the Gallit men had disappeared, Meg slipped quietly down the stairs of the main building and out one of the back doors that led to the nurses' quarters. She slowed as the Matron appeared ahead of her, along with three of the doctors.

As they met, Matron took Meg by the shoulders. "Meg! What's going on in there?"

"Gallit forces. They were looking for Prince Felipe. Cait tried to tell them he was gone, but now they've taken her!"

"Mother Above! Have they hurt anyone else?"

"A lot of the men are scared. They heard the gunfire and are reacting exactly as you'd expect. I don't know if there's enough of us to keep them all calm."

"Then why are you going this way?"

"I'll be back as soon as I can, Matron. I just need to get something from my room."

The Matron looked like she wanted to argue further, but one of the doctors tugged on her sleeve and she realised she couldn't spare the time.

"Be as quick as you can, Meg."

"Yes, Matron."

They parted ways and Meg ran the rest of the way

back to her room. Hattie had heard the noise and was full of questions, but Meg didn't answer very many. She was busy pulling out the spare set of clothes she had kept at the bottom of her bag for such occasions.

"Meg, what are you doing?" Hattie asked and then added, almost as incredulously, "Are those *trousers?*"

Meg shrugged as she pulled the trousers on under her skirt. "You never know when you might need a pair."

"Meg, are you planning on just walking out there and fighting them?"

"No," Meg said and when she looked at Hattie after pulling on the shirt, her eyes were bright. "I'm going to steal a horse and follow them."

"They could be miles away by the time you get a horse saddled."

"Who said anything about saddling?" When Hattie's response to this was to continue looking confused, Meg added, "Hattie, I grew up on a farm with five older brothers. I've been riding bareback since I was four. I only need a horse."

"But -"

"I'm not saying it will be comfortable, but I'll manage. They've taken Cait, Hattie. I have to find out where."

She laced up her boots and shoved some money into a bag which she then slung over one shoulder. She then moved to the window and pushed it up. She was just about to sling one leg over and climb out when Hattie grabbed her by the arm.

"Meg! What are you planning to do once you know where they've taken Cait? March home and go straight to the Prince and tell him?"

"Actually, yes." Meg paused, deciding how much to tell the other woman. "I said I grew up on a farm and that's the truth, but for the two years before I came here, I was on the staff at the palace. My uncle got me a position there. Remember how Prince Felipe was always running off?" Hattie nodded. "I was one of the ones who sent the guards in the wrong direction so he could get further away."

"You knew him before he came here."

"Not well. But enough that when Cait told him that she was enlisting here, he asked me to enlist too and make sure nothing happened to her. I was to inform him the second she was in any danger. I don't know what he was actually thinking he'd be able to do if he was still on the front when this happened, but one doesn't say no when the prince asks a favour."

"Why didn't you ever say anything?"

"Because he asked me not to. He didn't want Cait to know. I was to act like I'd never seen her before in my life."

"You had us all convinced."

"So now you understand why I have to follow them."

"What am I going to tell Matron when she realises that both you *and* Cait are gone?"

"I don't know. The truth? Cait was taken and I went to help rescue her." She flashed Hattie a grin and then nimbly jumped through the open window. Once she was on the other side, she turned back to Hattie. "I'll be all right," she said, "don't worry. See you soon."

She turned and began jogging in the direction of the small stable that was kept on the hospital compound, leaving Hattie to try to process not only the night's events but also all the information she had just received.

CHAPTER FOURTEEN

Cait's journey inside the wagon was long, bumpy and uncomfortable. At one stage they stopped for a while, and a plate with a few slices of cold roast beef was slid through the door to her, along with a mug of water. She was not let out, though. She took the opportunity while the wagon was still to stand up and pace around, working the stiffness out of her legs. She could hear the Gallit men talking outside, but the sound was too muffled for her to hear what they were saying.

Finally, the journey reached its end, and Cait was roughly pulled outside. The Gallit men were making their way into what looked like an abandoned hotel. The outside was run down, though the remnants of the name of the establishment remained. Inside, a staircase ran up several storeys, and on the first one Cait could see numbered doors.

The man who had been giving orders back at the hospital directed the person holding onto Cait to take her down a flight of stairs leading to a basement. Once there, Cait was shoved inside a small room at one end and the door was locked behind her. The room was dark and cold and Cait's nose wrinkled as she smelt mould growing on the walls. There were vents in the door, but they didn't allow much light through.

Cait didn't know how long she sat there in the dark before she heard footsteps outside the room. She heard a key inside a lock and saw the door swing open. A man walked into the room carrying a lantern. Cait blinked in the new light, trying to see a face.

"Well, here we are again, Caitlin," said the man, and Cait started as she recognised the voice.

"Doctor Brayden?" For a moment, Cait thought that he was perhaps there to help her. However, the way he drew himself up to his full height to stand over her made her realise this was not the case. "What are you doing here?"

"Instigating the final part of a plan that has been in motion for many months."

"I don't understand."

"Of course you don't. Allow me to explain. The men who brought you here are not part of the Gallit military. They follow their own code. Ever since the first Gallit-Nardowyn war, they have been looking for ways to take back the land the Nardowyn claimed in the aftermath, and seek revenge for the Gallit lives lost. Killing Prince Sebastian was their first move. The next move was to take Prince Felipe into our custody and use him to barter with King Gilles."

"Is the Gallit government a part of this?"

"Of course not. But I expect Prime Minister Johann will want to cooperate with us as well in the interests of keeping the peace with Nardowyn. Unfortunately, I was unable to get word to anyone in time to report that Prince Felipe had left; I'm sure you understand that I couldn't simply send a letter that could be intercepted. But with you here, I think the original plan can be easily reworked."

"That's how they knew who I was," Cait said. "You told them about me." Doctor Brayden nodded, but did not respond. "Prince Felipe had been in hospital for weeks,"

Cait continued. "Why wait so long?"

The doctor gave Cait a wry smile. "Some of our men were a little over-enthusiastic. The explosion that landed the Prince in hospital was only supposed to weaken him enough that we would be able to easily subdue him and bring him here. Instead they took out a few dozen men and nearly killed the Prince as well. Dead, he's no good to us. We needed to know he'd received adequate care before we came for him; we can't look after a half-dead man here."

Cait processed this information in silence. Everything Doctor Brayden told her made sense, in a horrifying sort of way. Ever since the first war between Gallit and Nardowyn over thirty years ago, there had been factions of the Gallit population who had remained indignant about the terms of the Gallit surrender, including the extra territory that Nardowyn took over. That was why King Gilles had introduced the National Service Act not long after he succeeded the throne. Since then the young men in the Kingdom had been ensuring that the border stayed where it was. There was also the matter of the compensation that Nardowyn insisted the Gallit people pay for the damages caused to both Nardowyn people and property. Cait knew from things that she'd read that the Gallit government had had to increase taxes significantly to meet the payments; she could understand why people would be bitter about that.

"What do you get out of it?" Cait asked the doctor next. "People don't tend to just turn traitor for the fun of it."

"For a start, this job pays a lot better than a position as an army doctor ever will."

"That's it? Money? You get paid twice as much as I do; you're in no position to complain!"

"We like to see that our informants are well-compensated," said the man who had been giving orders back at the hospital, entering the room and coming to stand alongside Doctor Brayden. He was an imposing figure. Cait stared at his boots to avoid meeting his gaze.

"May I introduce our leader, Simian?" Doctor Brayden said, and Cait looked up just enough to see the other man give a small, smug bow in her direction.

"As we speak, word is being sent to Prince Felipe in Nardowyn to tell him that we have you here," Simian said. "If the rumours about you and him are true, we shouldn't have to wait long for him to turn up."

"This plan is far from foolproof," Cait replied.

"We have a contingency plan," Simian said, "but that is a last resort. Anyway, enough of that, it won't do for a prisoner to know all the ins and outs of our plans. How are you feeling, Caitlin? Should I have someone send some food?"

The mention of food made Cait realise that she was indeed quite hungry. It had been quite some time since the food had been passed to her in the middle of their journey. It could well have been a full day or more since she'd last had a proper meal. She nodded, not wishing to continue any kind of conversation with Simian.

"Very well. Come, Doctor. I have something to discuss with you further." The two men turned and left the cellar, and the door was bolted behind them. Cait settled herself back against the wall, wondering how long she was going to be left alone this time.

The next few days passed slowly for Cait. She had nothing to pass the time and the only way to tell whether it was night or day was whether it was bread and water that got passed through the door for breakfast or a bowl of bland stew for dinner. She had not been granted so much as a pillow so sleeping was difficult and when she was able to doze off, it was only for short periods of time. No one talked to her; she was of no interest to anyone there beyond her use as bait for Prince Felipe.

It was the fifth night she had been there when she

awoke with a crick in her neck to the sounds of yelling and gunfire. Most of it was far away, but she could hear Simian's voice barking orders as it became gradually closer. She jumped as a shot sounded right outside her cell and the door swung open, the lock in pieces. Without a word, Simian marched over to Cait and grabbed her roughly by one arm, pulling her to her feet. He gave her a shove towards the door.

"Move."

"You're hurting me."

"You'll live." Simian paused and gave a small chuckle. "Well... that remains to be seen."

As they moved through the corridor outside the cell and up a flight of stairs, Cait felt unsettled by that last remark. She was distracted a moment later by the sight of men - in both the black uniform of Simian's group and the red of the Nardowyn Royal Guard - lying dead or injured. They could be found both on the stairs and along the one main corridor from the front room they were now in. She could hear voices from both the corridor and up above, calling out to each other and, she realised, calling out her name as well.

Simian manoeuvred Cait so that she was slightly in front of him, and then Cait felt the barrel of his pistol in her back.

"Is this what you're looking for, Your Highness?" he called out loudly. The shouting upstairs quieted slightly, and the faces of a few Nardowyn guards bent over the railing. There were footsteps from the corridor and squinting, Cait realised that Prince Felipe had been either stupid or stubborn enough to insist on coming there himself, just as Simian and his men had hoped. Her heart gave another jolt when Meg appeared next to him. What in the world was she doing there?

Prince Felipe leaned on his cane as he stopped walking and took in the sight of Cait and Simian in the entrance hall before him. Initially, relief had washed over his face when he saw Cait, but it was quickly replaced by concern as he took in her situation.

"Cait, are you all right?"

"That depends on you, Your Highness," Simian replied before Cait had a chance to say anything. "I've got one shot left but I'm willing to trade with you. Give yourself up and Caitlin goes free. Then I'll only use this shot to make sure you can't walk back out of here."

As Cait watched, the Prince seemed to consider Simian's offer for a few moments. He then began to walk slowly towards them. Every step echoed in Cait's ears and her awareness of both Simian's grip on her arm and cold metal on her back seemed to heighten as she waited.

Once he was close enough, Felipe regarded Simian with a cold stare. He held up the hand without the cane, palm outward, to show that he was unarmed. His eyes never left Simian's face.

"Felipe, what are you doing?" While Cait would of course have not preferred to be there, she was terrified by the thought that Felipe would agree to Simian's terms so easily to ensure her safety.

"It's the only way, Cait."

"What? No! There has to be another way! Something else we can do!"

"Cait..."

"Don't you see they'll just kill you, too?" Cait's voice caught on the lump that had formed in her throat.

By this time Felipe was only an arm's length away from her and Simian. He finally dropped his eyes to meet her gaze. "I'm sorry, Cait."

The next second passed in a blur. Cait opened her mouth to try to argue again, but was cut off by the impact of a blow the prince himself dealt to her head with a weapon he seemingly produced from nowhere. She fell sideways, dimly aware of Simian cursing and of more shots being fired, but then her head hit the wall and everything went black.

CHAPTER FIFTEEN

Prince Felipe chose not to dwell on the uncomfortably loud crack with which Cait's head hit the wall as she fell. He instead focused on the fact that he had also managed to shoot Simian in the shoulder, rendering the insurgent's dominant arm useless and sending him reeling back against the wall. From here, he slumped to the ground.

"Where the hell did that come from?" Simian growled, nodding towards the pistol still in the Prince's hand. He held his own hand up to his wound in a fruitless attempt to stem the blood flow.

"If I had been wearing the sort of royal garb I've been forced into most of my life, or even the army uniform, I'm sure you would have immediately assumed that I had a weapon concealed somewhere," the Prince replied. "But I was in a hurry when I left home, you see, and I wasn't dressing for the occasion. It worked to my advantage, though, didn't it? Because while my hands were raised you never suspected I had a gun hidden in the back of the trousers. My leg may have been injured but my arm's still as quick as it ever was. They train us well in the Nardowyn military. It's no wonder we keep winning the wars."

"You haven't won this one yet."

"No, but the odds do seem to be in our favour."

Simian scowled but did not reply. His focus had turned to trying to stem the blood flow from his injured shoulder. Prince Felipe looked around and beckoned to a couple of his men.

"Pick him up. We don't want him bleeding out before his trial."

As the two Nardowyn men moved towards Simian, he made a grab for his pistol where it had fallen a few paces away from him. Unfortunately for him, it was closer to Prince Felipe, who barely had to move his foot in order to kick it out of Simian's reach.

The Prince's men hoisted Simian back to his feet. One of them had paused to pull the shirt off one of the fallen men and balled it up, using it to apply pressure to Simian's wound.

"That should do to stop the bleeding," he said and Prince Felipe nodded in acknowledgement before turning to another of his men.

"Gather up as many of our men as are still standing. Patch up the injured as best you can. The Gallits as well. They will all stand trial. Lock them somewhere in here until I return."

"Yes, sir," the soldier replied before going off in search of his comrades.

The Prince looked back up the corridor he had been down when he had heard Simian call out to him and realised Meg was still there. She had one had on a wall to support herself and was looking pale. Prince Felipe made his way back towards her.

"Meg..."

"What did you do?" Meg's eyes were darting between him and Cait's still body lying against the wall back in the entrance hall.

"Meg, I was..."

"She's my friend! I thought you wanted to help her!"

"I did, Meg! And I have!"

"What? How?"

"There was no way I could get to Simian while he was holding her there. He would have shot her." He glanced back at Cait and a guilty expression passed across his face. "I had to hurt her to save her."

Meg's expression became less frantic as she processed Prince Felipe's words and realised what his plan had been. She looked over at Cait once more. "Will she be all right?"

"I think so. I hope so. Will you help me get her out of here, Meg?"

Meg nodded, and they made their way back towards the entrance hall. Meg bent down and hooked one of Cait's arms around her neck, pulling her into a standing position. Prince Felipe was then able to hook Cait's other arm around his own neck. Her head rolled from side to side. There was already a lump forming on her temple. They moved slowly, as the Prince had to alternate between leaning on his cane and then on Cait and Meg, but eventually they manoeuvred Cait out of the building. While most of his men, and Meg, had ridden horses, his leg had prevented him from doing so as well and so a carriage was waiting outside. The driver hopped down to help load Cait into it.

"Meg, you stay with her," the Prince said. "I'll have someone take care of your horse. I'll be back in a moment."

Meg nodded and climbed into the carriage. Prince Felipe turned to the driver and gave him directions before walking back into the building. His men had found a few more of Simian's and had herded them down to the basement. Two Nardowyn guards were standing on the stairs, preventing escape. Prince Felipe chose a couple of men to be in charge, explained to them where he was taking Cait and that Meg's horse would need looking after, and then made his way back outside. He climbed into the carriage and then knocked on the roof with his cane to indicate to the driver he was ready to go. The carriage began to move and he sat back, hoping he hadn't hurt Cait too badly.

Cait felt the sunshine on her face before she opened her eyes. She was lying in a bed far more comfortable than the one she had been used to for the past several months, and her head was nestled in a plump pillow. When she opened her eyes, she saw that she was in a big room with a tall ceiling and glass doors that opened out onto a spacious courtyard. There was a vase of flowers on the bedside chest to her left and when she turned her head, she saw two plush armchairs sitting along the wall to her right. Prince Felipe was sitting in one of them, his cane leaning on one arm of it. He had fallen asleep, his chin on his chest. Cait wondered how long he had been sitting there, waiting for her to wake up.

"Good morning," she said loudly, and it was enough for the Prince's eyes to spring open.

"Cait!" He stood up quickly and then stumbled as he remembered he still needed his cane to walk. He eased himself back into the chair, looking sheepish. Cait smiled.

"How are you feeling?" he asked.

As Cait tried to remember how she had ended up there, she became aware of a dull throbbing in her head. She raised her hand to her temple and ran it across a lump that had formed there.

"You hit me," she said, the memory of the shock coming back to her.

She looked at the Prince again; her smiled had faded. Prince Felipe did not meet her eyes.

"Cait..."

"I could have been shot!"

"I know... but I had to take that risk."

"What?"

"Cait, hurting you was the one thing that Simian didn't expect me to do. It bought me time, and I was able to get you out of immediate danger. Whether I'd gone with him like he wanted, or refused, you would have been killed. I had to think of something else."

Cait processed this in silence, while Prince Felipe picked at a loose thread in the upholstery on the arm of his chair so that he didn't have to make eye contact with her. Finally, Cait said, "It was a big risk."

"I know," Felipe replied quietly.

"You had no guarantee I'd be safe."

"I didn't."

There was another silence. "But it did work." A small, hopeful smile appeared on the prince's face. "Though my head still hurts," Cait added playfully, returning the smile. Prince Felipe laughed, and he seemed to relax. Cait found she couldn't stay angry at him for long. He had, after all, gotten her out of that horrible place eventually, even if there had been risks involved.

"Where are we?" she asked, wanting to move the subject to something they would not argue about.

"This is the Prime Minister's official residence," Felipe explained. "That hideout Simian and his men had wasn't actually far from here, and when you were hurt I didn't want to just take you to some hotel. The staff here sent for a doctor right away. This morning Prime Minister Johann sent out a group of Gallit men to bring in Simian and his band. And I've sent word to my father; there's no need for the war to go on now that we know who's responsible for Sebastian's death."

"It's over then?"

"It soon will be. Prime Minister Johann is writing up orders for the Gallit army as we speak."

"That's wonderful."

"Yes." They lapsed into silence, and once again Felipe fidgeted with the arm of his chair. When the silence got too long he looked up again and said, "Cait... what I said... the night before I left..."

Cait felt a knot quickly form in the pit of her stomach. "Please, let's not talk about that just now," she interrupted.

"What was Meg doing there? At the hideout with you?"

The Prince didn't answer at first, clearly uneasy about Cait's avoidance of the subject. "She enlisted to be a nurse at my behest. When you told me you'd signed up, I... I wanted to make sure you were safe. Or that I had someone who could let me know if you weren't."

"What were you going to do about me from the front?"

Felipe shrugged. "I didn't really think that far."

"But how did you know her before? Did she work for you?"

"She was on our staff, yes. I often saw her in the gardens. In fact, it's partly thanks to her that we met at all. That day at the festival. She helpfully put the guards off my track until I had a chance to blend in with the rest of the crowd."

Cait smiled, remembering that day and realising how much her opinion of Felipe had changed since then. "If the war is essentially over, will I be going back to the hospital? Or straight back home?"

"I've arranged for you to go home tomorrow. I hope you don't mind. I could have that changed, though, if you did want to go back to your work. The hospitals are going to be emptying at a slower rate than the trenches. Some of our men still need good care, and not all of them can be moved yet."

Cait gently prodded at the lump on her temple again. It was still throbbing. "I think I've had enough excitement to last me a while. I'm quite happy to go home. What about my things, though? I take it they're still at the hospital."

"I'll arrange for someone to fetch them."

At that moment, a particularly sharp stab of pain emanating from her wound shot through Cait's head and she gasped, her hand flying to the spot on her temple. Felipe immediately stood up, remembering his cane this time.

"Are you all right? Should I send for the doctor now?"

Cait grimaced. "I think I'm all right. But yes, please

do."

Felipe nodded and made his way out the room. Cait settled herself back into the sheets. The pain in her head started to dull again, but she decided that while ever she could use it as an excuse to stay in bed, she would. It was a long time since she had been able to sleep in.

Cait was brought lunch in her room, which she sat up to eat, and then the doctor came to examine her head once more. He asked her a few questions about how she was feeling, and then a few more to ensure that her faculties were still intact. He pronounced that there was no lasting damage as far as he could tell, and that she was fit for travelling home.

None of her clothing was available to her. Someone had taken the clothes she had spent her entire imprisonment in, and dressed her in something clean, so she borrowed a simple dress from one of the maids to wear for the rest of the day. She was also given a couple more for her journey home. She promised she would have them returned as soon as possible.

Cait spent the rest of the day talking to Meg. Once the doctor had seen her she was allowed to get up and about, so they spent some time in the gardens. The Prime Minister's residence was built in a rectangle, with most of the rooms on the ground floor opening up onto the quadrangle in the middle. In the centre of the quadrangle was an enormous oak tree that towered over the rest of the building. As far as Meg had been able to establish, the tree held no great significance, but it had been deemed too beautiful to merely cut down to make way for more buildings. Hence the architect had found a way to accommodate it.

Cait and Meg sat at a small table under this tree and drank afternoon tea while they caught up. Meg talked about her time working in the palace before she enlisted to be a nurse, and how she had known Prince Felipe. She also confided in Cait how horrified she had been as she watched the Prince hit Cait with his gun. She had thought that perhaps *he* had been the one who turned traitor, right under their noses, and that she and the Nardowyn men that had come with them were about to end up dead as well. Even when he had explained his plan, she had still been anxious about it.

That evening, Meg and Cait were invited to dine with the Prime Minister, his wife and Prince Felipe. Prime Minister Johann and the Prince dominated most of the conversation, speaking in political and military jargon that Cait didn't quite follow. From the sounds of it, word had come that King Gilles would be on his way to Gallit the following day, and that the proper negotiations to end the war could begin once he arrived.

Cait retired to her room soon after dinner. Though she had apparently been unconscious for quite some time after her knock to the head, the events of the past few days were still wearing on her, and she became tired quite early. She tried to read one of the books sitting on the bedside chest, but found herself nodding off to sleep, and eventually gave in to the temptation.

The following morning, Cait said goodbye to Meg and Prince Felipe, and was driven away in a waiting carriage. She recognised the inn they stopped at that night as the same one that she had stayed at on the day she left home.

The next afternoon, when the carriage came to a stop outside her home, Cait thanked the driver and then hurried up the stairs and knocked on the door. She had to wait for a few minutes until it was opened. It was Sophie who answered and it took a moment for her to register who she was looking at.

"Hello, Sophie," Cait said, "I'm home a bit early."

"It's good to see you, Miss," she said. "We weren't expecting you."

"Are Mother and Ginny home? I imagine Father is still at work, but I hoped I might see the two of them."

"Yes, Miss, they are. Come on in."

Sophie led her to the sitting room. Through the door, Cait could see her mother sitting on one of the sofas and going through the day's mail.

"Miss Caitlin, Ma'am," Sophie announced.

Cait's mother looked up in surprise, dropping the envelope in her hand.

"Thank you, Sophie," Cait said quietly, and Sophie bustled away, leaving room for Cait to move into the room.

"Hello, Mother," she said. Her mother stood up and quickly moved towards her, her arms outstretched.

"You're home early," she said, holding Cait in a tight embrace. "I mean, with the war ending, we were hoping it would be soon, but then we hadn't heard from you..."

"I'm sorry," Cait replied. "I should have written. I have a lot to fill you in on." She pulled out of her mother's embrace and sat down in an adjacent chair. "Let me tell you everything."

CHAPTER SIXTEEN

It was a fortnight later when word spread that Prince Felipe and King Gilles were finally on their way home from Gallit. There was still work to be done, treaties to be written and signed by both parties. But the war was effectively over and both sides were pulling their troops out of the combat zone.

Cait didn't know what to expect when she heard the news. Her rational side knew that Felipe was probably busy with state business and affairs such as his daughter's Naming Ceremony, but she still found herself wanting to see him and make sure he was looking after himself.

As it turned out, she only had to wait three days to find out. She had just returned home after picking Ginny up from school when there was a knock at their door. Sophie opened it and appeared in the sitting room a little while later, clearing her throat to get Cait's attention.

"Prince Felipe to see you, Miss." She sounded as though that was not an announcement she had ever expected to make.

Cait stood up quickly, but then tried to conceal her

haste. "It's good to see you," she said. "Please, come in and sit down." Prince Felipe nodded his thanks to her, and then moved into the room and sat in the chair Cait motioned to.

At first, neither of them knew what to say, until Cait broke the silence by asking, "How did your dealings with the Prime Minister go?"

"Very well. Both forces are basically out of the war zone now. Men are returning home everywhere."

"That's good to hear."

Prince Felipe continued, "I believe there is to be a parade soon, to celebrate the army's return to Nardowyn."

"I suppose Ginny will insist on a roadside spot for that."

"Probably," the Prince agreed.

Ginny was bound to be excited to greet all the soldiers returning home. For Cait, having seen so many injuries and so much death while she worked at the hospital meant she couldn't help but imagine how such a parade would affect those families who had lost someone. She thought of Ava and Bridget. She had been to see them not long after she had returned home and it had been clear that although they were doing well on the surface, the pain of losing their brother was still raw.

"How's your leg?"

Felipe shrugged, his smile fading a little. "The pain comes and goes now. Sometimes I can barely stand on it, other times it feels fine. The sooner I can get rid of the cane, the better, though."

"You'll get there eventually."

"How is your family? Were they surprised when you got back?"

"They were. It took quite a while to persuade my mother to let go of me."

Prince Felipe laughed and looked on the verge of saying something else when Sophie knocked on the door frame.

"I'm sorry for interrupting, Your Highness, but we were wondering if you were planning on staying for dinner?"

Felipe glanced at Cait and then back to Sophie. "As long as I won't be any trouble."

"Of course you won't," Cait assured him. "Thank you, Sophie." The maid nodded and disappeared again.

Dinner was still an hour away, so Cait and Prince Felipe chatted until then. Cait's father arrived home from the university and stuck his head into the sitting room to greet his eldest daughter. Cait introduced him to Felipe, and they shook hands before her father excused himself to prepare for dinner.

Over roast lamb, Felipe talked happily with all of Cait's family, and she was pleased to see them all hit it off so well. Ginny did ask one or two questions about the war that caused the Prince's eyes to cloud over while certain memories came back to him. Cait quickly steered the conversation in a different direction, and for the most part, the conversation was quite cheerful.

The Prince asked James about his work at the university. Prince Sebastian had been studying for twelve months before he left on National Service, and had intended to finish his degree once he returned. Felipe didn't consider himself hugely academic, but he supposed the option was always there.

When dinner was finished, Prince Felipe asked Cait's father if they could speak in private. Cait's heart sped up as she felt all three of her family members glance at her. No doubt they were wondering why the Prince would make such a request. She hadn't mentioned Felipe's proposal the night before he left the hospital; there had been so much else to talk about and to be honest, she didn't want to answer questions about why she had said no.

Cait considered going up to her room, but talked herself into waiting downstairs while her father and Felipe disappeared into her father's study.

"Cait, what in the world is making you so nervous?" her mother asked at one point.

"I'm not nervous," Cait replied automatically, but her mother raised her eyebrows and glanced down at Cait's hands. When she looked down at them herself, she realised she was wringing them tightly.

"I just..." she stammered. "I just don't know what they'd be talking about and I wish I did."

"Don't you?" her mother replied, smiling gently. "Because I think I could hazard a guess."

Cait felt her face turn red, and didn't respond.

Fifteen minutes later, her father and the Prince emerged from the study. Cait, Ginny and their mother met the two men in the hall outside the sitting room. When Felipe met Cait's eyes, his expression was almost bashful.

"May I speak with you again, Cait, before I leave?"

Cait saw her parents share a meaningful look, and then her mother hustled Ginny away, leaving the sitting room free for Cait and the prince. They each sat back down on the chairs they had been using before dinner. Cait waited for Felipe to say something, but suddenly he was shy.

"What did you want to speak to me about?" Cait prompted, not wanting the awkward silence to go on any longer.

Prince Felipe took a deep breath. "Every time I try to talk about this, you end up changing the subject," he said. "The night before I left... I might not have admitted it at the time, but you were right. That wasn't the time to say any of the things I said... but that doesn't make them any less true." He paused for a moment to gauge Cait's reaction; she was keeping her expression as neutral as possible, but she nodded for him to continue. "And, well, you never did exactly say that your feelings for me were any different from those I have for you..."

At this point, he held out his hands to Cait, and when she gave him hers, he clasped them tightly. "Cait, I think I fell in love with you the day I met you, when you scolded me for skipping the lunch I was supposed to have been at. Do you remember?"

Cait couldn't help smiling at the memory. "I was so determined to dislike you at the time."

"I know that I put you through a lot that I shouldn't have, and I also know that I am far from perfect and that you will probably always find me frustrating, but if you can look beyond all that... Cait, would you do me the honour of being my wife?"

Even having suspected that the question was coming, Cait still felt her stomach twist into a knot when she heard it. Regardless of her feelings for Felipe, the prospect of the life that would come with being his wife terrified her.

"Does your father know about this?" she asked, buying herself some time before she had to give him a proper answer. "Doesn't he have another princess lined up for you?"

Felipe scoffed. "He'd like to think so. But I've already told him, I did my duty by marrying Maria. This time I get to make the choice."

"And doesn't your heir need to be of noble blood? On both sides of his family?"

"Well, in a few months that shouldn't matter. I'm petitioning to have the line of succession laws changed so that the eldest child of the reigning monarch will inherit the throne regardless of gender." Cait's eyes widened, which prompted Felipe to keep going. "The more I thought about your arguments on the subject, the more I realised they made much more sense than any of our current laws... but I never would have thought about it at all if not for you."

"I take full credit," Cait said, unable to help the huge smile that had spread across her face.

"And now you've done it again, Cait, distracting me with another subject. But please just tell me yes or no, the suspense is killing me."

With that, he looked at Cait with an expression so

imploring that it was enough to make Cait forget all the reasons she had planned on giving him for why marrying her was a bad idea. She leaned forward and squeezed his hands, which she was still holding.

"My answer is yes," she said.

Prince Felipe's sigh of relief was audible as he sat back in his chair. "I thought you might have been leading up to turning me down again," he said. "And honestly, I don't know what I would have done then."

"I think I made some good points when I turned you down," Cait said, smirking.

"Oh, I agree completely. I do now, anyway. I was furious with you at the time."

Cait didn't respond to that, but her smirk remained. "May I tell my family about this? Or do I have to wait for an official announcement?"

"Your immediate family can know, of course. Just... try to impress upon Ginny that no one else should know until it's official.."

This made Cait laugh, but she nodded. "I'll make sure she understands."

"It might be a little while before we can announce anything. I'm probably supposed to still be in mourning."

"Well, as you said the first time you tried proposing to me, we don't have to get married next week."

Felipe nodded. "Exactly." He glanced towards the door. "Shall we tell your parents now?"

Cait nodded. "Yes. I think I'd like for you to be here when I tell them."

They stood up and Felipe offered Cait the arm that wasn't holding his cane. They found her parents and Ginny sitting around their dining table. They all looked up expectantly when Cait and Felipe came into the room.

Ginny, always one for cutting straight to the chase, immediately asked with a grin from ear to ear, "Are you getting married, then?"

Ellen laid a hand on Ginny's to quiet her but Cait

smiled. "As a matter of fact, we are, Ginny."

If Ginny's grin could have possibly got any wider, that was what happened as she squealed excitedly. Cait's mother stood and came around the table to give Cait a hug, which Ginny joined a moment later, while James shook Felipe's hand in congratulations. Ginny then hugged Felipe, though only for a second before she seemed to realise how close she was to the man whom she had swooned over pictures of for so long. Suddenly she became very shy. Ellen was less star-struck when it was her turn, and gave him a kiss on the cheek, a gesture he returned with a smile.

"I'm afraid I really must be on my way home," Felipe said once all the congratulations and embraces were done, and once he had explained about the official announcement that would eventually come from the palace. "I hadn't intended to be away this long and I didn't send any word; my father probably thinks I'm back to my old tricks and running away again. Cait, will you come and see me tomorrow afternoon so I can introduce you to my parents?"

"Of course. I'll walk you to the door."

"I'm so glad to meet you all," Felipe said, nodding to Cait's parents and to Ginny.

"Goodnight, Your Highness," Ellen replied, and the other two nodded in farewell. Cait took Felipe's hand and together they walked back towards the entrance hall.

"Until tomorrow, then," Felipe said, raising Cait's hand to his lips and kissing it lightly.

"Until tomorrow," Cait agreed.

CHAPTER SEVENTEEN

The following morning, Cait and her mother went into the city as soon as the shops were open, searching for something appropriate for Cait to wear when meeting the King and Queen. Ellen muttered about there not being enough time to have something made specially, but Cait replied she was sure the King and Queen would understand, given how quickly everything was happening.

They returned home two hours later with a blue dress and an ornate gold comb for Cait's hair. Once she was dressed, she sat down at the dressing table and Ellen did her usual battle with Cait's curls, finally winning and securing the comb in a prominent spot. When she was done, she turned Cait towards her and pinched her cheeks to give them some colour.

"There," she said when she was done. "Beautiful."

Cait smiled and took her mother's hands in hers, squeezing them tightly. "I'm getting married," she said, still not quite believing it, "to a prince!"

"I know," her mother replied. "Who would have believed it?"

Not long after, Cait was on her way to the palace. She had only ever felt nervous on this trip once before, when she and Felipe had first started getting along properly. Before now, the likelihood of meeting any members of the Royal Family other than Prince Felipe had always been very slim. This time she was travelling there with the express purpose of meeting the King and Queen, and from what Felipe had said the previous day, the King was not entirely sold on the idea of his son marrying a commoner.

Felipe met Cait at the stairs, and a smile spread over his face the moment they made eye contact. "You look stunning," he said, kissing her hand again when she met him at the top of the stairs.

Cait blushed. "I wish I'd had more time to find an appropriate outfit."

"You know you could turn up here wearing a potato sack and I'd still be pleased to see you."

"It's not *you* I'm worried about impressing."

"You have nothing to worry about with my mother. She is eager to meet you. As for my father, he is a stickler for tradition but his bark is worse than his bite. Just be yourself, Cait, and everything will be fine."

"I hope you're right."

Felipe led her to a part of the palace she'd never seen before, and knocked on a tall, wooden door.

"This is my mother's suite," he explained as they waited for an answer from within. A servant opened the door and on seeing Felipe there, stepped aside to allow him and Cait entry. Cait could hear music and looking further into the room, saw that it was in fact Queen Juliette herself sitting at a harp, fingers moving deftly across the strings. She was sitting with her back to the door, and was unaware that she had company.

Felipe waited until she finished the piece she was playing and then walked up behind her, placing a hand on each of her shoulders and bending to kiss her cheek. She jumped in surprise, and then realising who it was behind her, placed one hand on his and turned around.

"Felipe, you scared me half to death."

"I'm sorry," Felipe replied. "I've got someone for you to meet." He beckoned to Cait for her to join him and his mother. "Mother, this is Caitlin," he said. "She's the woman I'm going to marry."

Queen Juliette smiled and offered her hand to Cait, who shook it. "Pleased to finally meet you, my dear," the Queen said. "I've been hearing all about you. I'm sure the two of you will be very happy together."

"I hope so, Your Majesty."

They spoke for a little longer. Cait asked the Queen about her music and the Queen asked Cait about her family. Cait found that it was very easy to forget she was speaking to the wife of the country's reigning monarch.

Finally, though, Queen Juliette said, "Well, Felipe, you'd better take Cait to meet your father before it gets too late," and Cait felt all her earlier nerves return in an instant.

The Queen must have seen Cait's face pale, because she put an assuring hand on Cait's arm. "Don't worry, Cait. He may be intimidating but you'll be fine."

"That's what Felipe told me. I hope you're both right."

"You've got nothing to worry about," Felipe said again, taking her hand. "Mother, I'll see you at dinner."

Cait gave the Queen a small wave as Felipe led her out of the suite and along another series of unfamiliar corridors.

"Don't worry, you'll know your way around here soon enough," Felipe promised her. "Oh, look, just in good time."

A group of well-dressed men were coming out of a room ahead. They were talking quietly amongst themselves and shuffling wads of paper around. King Gilles brought up the rear, thanked the men for coming and told them they would discuss matters further at a later date. He moved to head off further down the hall, but Felipe called out to him and he turned back. Felipe held Cait's hand tightly as he closed the space between them and his father.

"Father, this is Caitlin," he said.

The King did not immediately reply, so Cait said, "Pleased to meet you, Your Majesty." She bowed slightly, hoping she was doing the right thing and not making herself look foolish. What she would have given to have been able to spend some time learning the proper etiquette before being thrown into all of this!

"I am pleased to meet you, too, Caitlin," the King replied. "Though I'm sure you'll understand why I am somewhat wary of my son's attachment to you."

"Father..."

"I did try to talk him out of it," Cait said quickly, "but, well, he was persistent."

Felipe looked scandalised, but Cait saw a glint in the King's eye and knew she had said the right thing.

"That sounds like him," the King agreed.

"Now, listen, I didn't bring Cait here so the two of you could conspire against me!"

"We're doing no such thing," Cait replied, her nervousness beginning to ease as she linked her arm in Felipe's and gave it a squeeze.

"Of course not," the King agreed.

An attendant appeared from further up the hall and cleared his throat. "Your Majesty, I'm sorry for interrupting, but another letter has arrived from the Treasury."

The King sighed. "Just when I thought I was done for the day." He looked at Felipe and Cait apologetically. "I'm afraid I can't spare more time just now," he said. "Duty calls. Felipe, if you are sure about this wedding, then come and see me tomorrow and we'll discuss it further."

"Will you be at dinner tonight?"

The King waved the letter, which he had taken from the attendant, as though that answered the question. "Who knows?"

Felipe frowned slightly. "Well, tomorrow, then."

The King nodded, and then looked at Cait. "Miss Caitlin. I'm sure we'll meet again."

"I'm sure we will, Your Majesty."

With that, the King turned on his heel and stalked away. Felipe turned to Cait, a broad smile on his face. "See? I told you had nothing to worry about."

"He still doesn't seem entirely convinced."

"No, but he's also not entirely *unconvinced*. Don't worry. I'll talk to him tomorrow and make him see that he hasn't really got any choice in the matter."

"Your optimism really is endearing. What now?"

"Well, there's still one person for you to meet."

"Who?"

"You'll see."

He took her hand and began walking again. When they arrived at their destination, he pushed open the door and Cait realised they were in a nursery. Of course, who else would he have wanted her to see but his daughter?

A wet nurse was sitting in a rocking chair near a bassinet, holding a bundle of blankets and whispering to it. Cait hung back by the door but could hear gurgles coming from under the blankets as Felipe crossed the room.

"Elizabeth," he greeted the nurse. "May I?"

"Of course," she replied. "Careful, though, she's just gone to sleep." She manoeuvred the baby into the Prince's arms and then he crossed the room back to Cait.

"Cait, may I introduce Maria?" he said.

"She's beautiful," Cait said, looking down to see a small, chubby face sleeping peacefully. "Maria?"

"We thought it was fitting," Felipe replied. "Of course, in true Royal Family tradition, she has half a dozen other names following it, but we needn't worry about those for now. Would you like to hold her?"

Cait nodded, and Felipe passed the tiny princess over to her. "It's a shame she'll never know her mother," Cait said quietly.

"Yes," Felipe agreed, "but... she'll know you."

Cait look up from where she had been stroking the baby's cheek. "I never thought I'd be mother to the future queen."

Felipe placed a hand on her arm and leaned over to kiss her forehead. "You won't be alone. There will be plenty of people to help you." He turned and motioned to the nurse, who came and took the baby from Cait's arms, and then he took her hand again. "Will you stay for dinner? Your family hosted me last night; I'd like to return the favour. If it helps to persuade you, my father probably won't be present."

Cait laughed. "I'd love to, even if your father is there."

To pass the time until dinner was to be served, Felipe took Cait on a tour of parts of the palace she hadn't seen before. As they walked, Cait tried keeping track of all the twists and turns they took, but eventually decided that was something that would only come with time.

When dinner time arrived, Felipe led her to the dining room and pulled out a chair for her across from his own. Cait stared at the array of plates, glasses and cutlery in front of her, trying to remember if she was supposed to work inward or outward with the knives and forks; it had been a long time since she had been to a university dinner with her father, and she always had trouble remembering. In the end, she just waited until Queen Juliette arrived and the first course was placed in front of them. Then she surreptitiously watched Felipe to see which implement he picked up first.

Though Felipe and the Queen were clearly used to it, to Cait it felt strange having so many people standing around the table, watching her eat. There was one man waiting to refill her wine glass should she so desire, another to dish out more meat and two more for the different vegetables. More staff trundled trolleys in and out with subsequent courses, taking empty dishes with them when they left.

After their meal, Felipe called for a carriage to be sent for Cait and walked her to the door. "I probably won't see you for a little while now," he said. "We probably shouldn't be seen together until after the official announcement. I'll let you know when that's going to be, because afterward, your life is probably going to get very hectic for a while. Everyone is going to want to know everything about you, and your family as well, probably. I'll have a guard posted at your house to keep the worst of them at bay, though you'll probably be spending a fair amount of time here anyway, so with luck there won't be too much to worry about."

Unable to resist, Cait looked at him seriously and said, "I hope you're worth it." The look he gave her indicated that he wasn't sure if she was serious or joking, so she smiled and leaned up to kiss him on the cheek. "I'm sure you will be," she assured him. His face relaxed into a smile.

"Your carriage awaits," he said, motioning dramatically as it appeared at the bottom of the stairs. He took a step closer to her and returned the kiss on the cheek. "Goodnight, Cait."

"Goodnight."

CHAPTER EIGHTEEN

It was another month before the Royal Family felt prepared to announce Felipe's engagement to Cait publicly, and as Felipe had warned, Cait's life became hectic almost immediately. There were meetings with dressmakers to design not only Cait's wedding dress, but also dresses for royal receptions and other events before and after the wedding. As a commoner, Cait had to attend etiquette lessons, and was required to memorise the names of the members of the extended Royal Family. She was sure she would never remember it all.

As he had promised, Felipe had a guard placed at Cait's family's house. The guard soon found his work was cut out for him and was eventually joined by another; budding young journalists found hiding places up and down Cait's street, and hid there with their cameras in the hopes of a small glimpse of the princess-to-be. Eventually Felipe insisted on Cait being given her own apartment near the palace so that she didn't have to venture outside so much. Being separated from everyone frustrated Cait almost as much, but she was able to wander the palace gardens when she needed fresh air, and her family were allowed to visit whenever they liked.

There were also meetings with wedding planners to discuss guests that Cait would like to invite to the ceremony; thankfully she had only a small extended family. Apart from Ava's family, she had only a few close friends including Hattie and Meg, so her decision was fairly easy. The Royal Family, on the other hand, was spending hours at a time trying to narrow down lists of nobles and foreign dignitaries to invite. There had been controversy surrounding some of the invitations (or lack thereof) to Felipe's wedding to Princess Maria, so they were trying to avoid these without creating more issues for themselves.

Finally, the day arrived. Cait was woken by her mother and was immediately surrounded by a group of attendants especially chosen to help her prepare. Her dress, with its several tulle petticoats and delicately beaded bodice, proved just as difficult to get into as it had when she had first had it fitted, but she was actually ready ahead of schedule.

Queen Juliette came to visit her in her room just before she was due to leave. "There is quite a crowd out there," she said. "They are very keen to see you."

Cait took a deep breath. "I hope I live up to their expectations."

The Queen took her arm and led her out of her room and down towards the entrance hall. "You will stun them, my dear," she said, as they paused behind the closed main doors. She let go of Cait's arm and Cait turned to see her mother, along with the other ladies who had helped her that morning.

Ellen came forward and took Cait in her arms; Cait felt her nerves ease almost instantly. "You have always been a princess to me," her mother murmured in her ear. "Now the rest of the world will see it, too." Cait felt her eyes well up and blinked furiously, giving her mother another squeeze to channel her emotions elsewhere. She only pulled away when the Queen gently touched her shoulder, telling her it was time to leave.

As the doors opened outward, a great roar went up from the crowd outside. Cait took another deep breath and then stepped forward, smiling at the people on the other side of the gate. She had no idea whether or not they could see it from the distance they were, but she had been taught that it was better to assume they could and to put on a show for them either way. She waved in the graceful way she had been shown. As the noise from the crowd got louder, she became more and more grateful for the gate between them, and wished that she did not have to pass through it to reach her destination.

She was assisted into the waiting carriage at the bottom of the stairs and, once her skirts and train had been arranged comfortably around her, they trundled off. She had feared that perhaps the crowds would not part to allow the carriage through, but she had enough guards surrounding her that this did not become a problem.

She waved to the crowds that lined the streets, paying special attention to the children; she remembered how excited Ginny had been when Felipe and Princess Maria had driven past her on their wedding day. It was hard to believe that was not even two years ago.

A red carpet had been laid out along the path from the end of the road to the marriage grotto so that Cait, Felipe and the wedding guests could get there without their shoes or clothes getting dirty. By the time Cait arrived, the guests had all arrived and were seated. As Cait's father led her up the aisle, she kept her eyes fixed on the bright green foliage overhanging the walkway. It was easier to focus on that than be tempted to make eye contact with all the people whose gazes were fixed on her. She felt nervous enough as it was.

Meeting Felipe at the top of the aisle did not necessarily calm her nerves, but Cait did feel somewhat relieved when he smiled at her and took her arm as her father slipped away. She kept her eyes on Felipe throughout the entire ceremony. Everything else about the day felt fuzzy around the edges, as though it was all a dream. But as long as she focused on Felipe, she knew this was really happening.

After so many weeks of preparation, the ceremony was over before Cait could believe it. The vows had all been said, the licences and certificates signed and she and Felipe were moving back down the aisle together as the guests on either side stood and clapped. Those sitting on the aisle reached out to congratulate them.

When they reached the main road again, what seemed like a hundred flashbulbs went off in their faces. Cait didn't think that there could possibly be enough newspapers in the kingdom to warrant that many photographers. Cait waved to the cheering crowd on the other side of the road and Felipe leaned on her slightly for support, then raised his cane in a sort of salute to the people. The cheers and whistles did not die down, but the Prince and new Princess had a schedule to keep, and they were soon ushered back into the carriage Felipe had travelled in to the marriage grotto.

As they began to move, Felipe leaned over to Cait and kissed her, much to the crowd's delight. Cait leaned into him at first, relishing the feeling of his lips on hers. Then she remembered how many pairs of eyes were on them and pushed him away; she was smiling, but her cheeks were pink. Felipe may have been used to being in the public eye, but she was still adjusting to it. Kissing in front of crowds was not something she felt she was really up to just yet.

As they continued, Cait and Felipe were turned away from one another as they waved to the people on their respective sides of the carriage, but Felipe found they could carry on a conversation despite this, and despite the noise.

"Apparently, the papers have been touting this as our 'fairytale wedding'," he said over his shoulder, "and I suppose they are right. But if this were a proper fairytale, I would have got to marry you right at the start."

Cait turned to face him and raised an eyebrow. "You think I would have made it that easy for you?"

Felipe laughed. "Of course not. Ours was always destined to be a more complicated fairytale."

Cait laughed with him and then leaned in to kiss him again despite her earlier reservations. When they broke apart again, she murmured in his ear, "And here's to a happily ever after that's just as interesting."

ABOUT THE AUTHOR

Emily has been writing since the age of six, but only recently developed the skill of finishing the projects that she starts (and even then, only sometimes). She is currently studying for a Masters in Museum and Heritage Studies and works at the National Library of Australia. In her spare time she can be found watching Doctor Who or curled up on the couch with a hot chocolate and a good book.

You can visit her blog for more information and links to all her other social media:
http://keysandopenmind.wordpress.com

Made in the USA
Charleston, SC
11 November 2016